SEXY
SAILORS

SEXY SAILORS
GAY EROTIC STORIES

EDITED BY
NEIL PLAKCY

CLEiS
PRESS

Published in the United States by Cleis Press, Inc., 2246 Sixth Street, Berkeley, California 94710.

Printed in the United States.
Cover design: Scott Idleman/Blink
Cover photograph: Rob Lang/Getty Images
Text design: Frank Wiedemann
First Edition.
10 9 8 7 6 5 4 3 2 1

Trade paper ISBN: 978-1-57344-822-2
E-book ISBN: 978-1-57344-836-9

Contents

INTRODUCTION

The British poet John Masefield wrote, "I must go down to the seas again, to the lonely sea and the sky." That poem expresses the yearning so many men have, to strike out for unknown waters in tall ships steered by stars. There's a romance to the water-borne life that comes from our longing to see new ports and to challenge ourselves in new ways.

From mariners on huge yachts to river boatmen to recreational boaters, the combination of men and water is irresistible. All the guys in this collection have fallen under the spell of the open water, and when you read their stories, you will, too. You'll sail from the canals of Britain to the crystal-blue tides of the Caribbean, from the ancient walled cities of Croatia to the San Francisco of the Gold Rush, and to many ports of call in between.

Masts, yardarms, jack lines—the language of sailors seems tailor-made for men who love men. Who hasn't admired a naval officer in his dress whites, or a lithe, tanned young man skimming across the water in control of a huge sail? And the water provides a convenient way to get men into (or out of!) tiny bathing suits as well.

The sexy sailors in this collection run from college boys seeking boyfriends to naval officers to older yachties with silver flecks in their hair. There are lots of well-worked muscles grinding winches to set and control sails, steer from the helm or tack to starboard as these stories veer from history to fantasy to present-day action.

Enjoy!

Neil Plakcy
October 2012

HOME IS
THE SAILOR

Emily Moreton

Danny! Hey, Danny, over here!"

It took Danny a second to figure out which direction the voice was coming from, the San Francisco dock being crowded with people. It didn't help that he had to squint into the bright sun just to make out individual faces. Even when he managed to zero in on the general area, it took a raised hand gesturing him over to pick out the exact person who'd called him.

"You made it!" Mike threw his arms around Danny in a suffocating hug the moment Danny was close enough. Danny returned the embrace as well as he could with his cane in one hand, drinking in the feel of Mike's warm, muscled body against his, the familiar smell of his deodorant and shampoo.

"Like I was going to stay away?" Danny drew back, taking in the man he'd been friends with since high school. Mike's hair was still as short and neat as Danny remembered it from college graduation two years before—he must have cut it in honor of coming into port—but he was darkly tanned, making his eyes seem startlingly bright. Standing next to him, Danny wondered if maybe he shouldn't have done more with his own blond hair than drag a comb through it. He definitely should have made more effort with his clothes—in jeans and an old UC San Francisco T-shirt, he really stood out amongst the uniforms. "You look good."

Mike laughed, warm and affectionate, same way he sounded on the phone calls that had been the only contact they'd had since Mike joined the navy right out of college. "Everyone looks good in uniform."

They were surrounded by Mike's fellow naval officers, by friends and family welcoming their boys and girls home, but the crowd provided a kind of anonymity, a secrecy. "You look really good," Danny said, low and quiet in Mike's ear, ducking his head to compensate for their slight height difference.

He felt Mike shiver, they were standing so close together. "Yeah?" Mike asked, looking over Danny's shoulder—at the huge ship, maybe, or at the ocean that had always captivated him.

"Hell, yeah," Danny agreed.

Someone pushed against him before he could say anything else, and for a second, his balance was a precarious thing. Mike's hand wrapped around his elbow in the same moment as Danny shifted his weight, leaning into the cane. Danny had to close his eyes, overwhelmed by the familiarity—the relief of having Mike home and close again.

"I've got you," Mike said quietly.

"I'm good."

Mike didn't let go, his hand hot against Danny's bare skin. "It's so good to see you," he said. "I wanted to—last time we got leave, I would have come."

Last time Mike had gotten leave, Danny had been up to his

eyeballs in his master's thesis, barely surfacing for food and water. He'd been the one to say that Mike should spend time with his family, instead of his friend with occasional benefits. It wasn't until a couple of weeks after Mike shipped out again that Danny had realized—and regretted—what he'd missed out on.

"You're here now," he said. "So, do I get to see this ship I've been hearing about?"

Mike made a weird face. "There's bits of it you can't go to because you're a civilian."

"Okay," Danny said gamely. He'd gotten used to hearing "it's classified" from Mike's mouth.

"And, um..." Mike actually shifted from one foot to the other, something he hadn't done since the time he'd told Danny he was joining the navy. "Most of it's not—with your cane, you won't be able to get around much."

It was an old hurt, now, being told he couldn't go somewhere because of his disability, worn soft with age, enough so that Danny could shrug it away. "Can you take me on deck?"

Mike's eyes drifted closed, just for a moment, his expression something Danny had never quite been able to read. It didn't entirely matter—he knew it meant that if they hadn't been in public, Mike would have kissed him. "I can do that," Mike agreed.

"I thought there'd be more people," Danny said when they made it on deck, most of the crowd left behind on the dock.

"Usually there are." Mike's bearing had shifted the moment they set foot on the ship, become more formal or something. He looked like he fit there in a way that made Danny very conscious of how Mike didn't quite fit on land anymore. "Most of the families come for the proper open session in a couple of days."

"So I'm a special case?"

"In so many ways," Mike teased. "No, we're allowed guests right now, it's just most people don't want to come up."

Danny'd seen enough home-from-war movies to figure that one out, even if Mike's ship hadn't actually been in any wars, just gone a long time. "Go on, then. Tell me a bit about this thing."

Mike, it turned out, knew a lot about the ship and its history. That didn't entirely surprise Danny—they'd met in AP History, after all—but he pretty quickly lost the thread of what Mike was saying. It didn't really matter. He didn't want to know the story behind the ship's name, or its dimensions, he just wanted to watch Mike talking about it and hear Mike's voice wash over him, be certain of Mike standing there, familiar and safe.

And, okay, maybe it was a little bit that listening to Mike, the sure, confident way he talked, was a pretty big, if unexpected, turn-on. Though it probably helped that Mike looked so damn good in his uniform.

What could Danny say? He'd watched a lot of old movies as a kid; apparently the whole dashing naval captain thing had seeped into his unconscious in ways he hadn't anticipated.

"You're staring," Mike said, sounding like he was about to laugh.

"I'm listening with rapt attention to what you're saying," Danny corrected.

"What was I just saying?"

"Something about...winches? I don't know, man, you started talking about getting your hands on a stiff piece of metal and working it, my mind took a short vacation."

It was hard to tell with Mike so tanned, but Danny thought he might be blushing. It was absurdly, adorably cute. "I was talking about equipment for keeping watch, actually."

"Does that include a periscope?" Danny asked innocently.

Mike cracked up. "And a telescope. Lots of telescopes."

"Are you keeping one in your pocket or are you just—"

"Happy to see me," Mike finished with him, still laughing. "I am."

"What, keeping a telescope in your pocket?" Danny eyed the tailored fit of Mike's uniform. "'Cause, honestly, it doesn't seem like you really have room."

"Happy to see you," Mike corrected patiently. His eyes flicked to Danny's crotch for a second, then back up to his face. "Happy to see a lot more of you."

"Well, you are here all week."

"Danny," Mike half groaned. "As much as I'd love to stand here and exchange witty banter all evening, I've been on a ship with no privacy for seven months. I haven't even jerked off in three weeks."

Danny bit down on the urge to ask if any of Mike's fellow sailors had taken care of him, not sure if he wanted to know the answer (possible extremely hot fantasy material) or not (possible extremely jealousy rendering material, especially if the guy was a friend of Mike's).

"What kind of friend would I be not to welcome the conquering hero home with proper honors?" He shifted slightly, his leg stiffening from staying in one position too long. "Come on, we can get a cab on the street."

Most of the cab drivers Danny'd dealt with were perfectly content to drive and ignore him. It was just his luck that, pressed thigh to thigh with Mike, sex a near prospect, he got one who wanted to talk.

Or, well, to be strictly accurate, Mike got one who wanted to talk. Danny was pretty much just along for the ride, so to speak.

"You came in on the *Louisiana*?"

"Yes, sir."

Danny rolled his eyes, not sure which of the two of them it was directed at. Next to him, Mike turned his hat slightly, resting it on his own left knee.

"Staying in town?"

"What, I'm invisible?" Danny muttered. Mike patted his knee and left his hand there, warm through the old denim, even when Danny shifted, trying to dislodge him.

"I am. My friend lives here."

The cab driver's eyes flicked to Danny in the rearview mirror for a moment, then dismissed him. "Always glad to have our boys in uniform in the city."

Danny rolled his eyes again. In response, Mike squeezed Danny's knee, making him jump slightly. He startled even more when Mike's hand traced up his thigh, coming to rest halfway up. "The hell are you doing?" he hissed.

"I've never spent much time here, I'm looking forward to a chance to get to know the city better," Mike said, like he wasn't feeling Danny up in the back of a cab while dressed in his full uniform.

Mike's fingers tickled the inside of Danny's thigh a little, making his other knee, the bad one, jump in response. Danny rested his own hand on it, trying to work out the misfiring nerves.

"I'll give you my card," the driver offered. "You need someone to show you around the city, give me a call."

Mike pressed his thumb into Danny's leg, his eyes intent on the driver's mirror. "Thanks for the offer, but I'm pretty sure Danny here will be playing tour guide."

Danny caught the driver eyeing him again, a look that said pretty clearly he'd be eyeing Danny's cane if it wasn't tucked down the side of the seat. He frowned back until the driver looked away. "Or, you know, a cab anywhere. Restaurant or something."

Mike squeezed Danny's leg hard enough to make him gasp, more than just his bad knee twitching with the contact. "I'll bear it in mind," he said. "But I think we'll mostly be eating in."

Danny pressed a hand over his mouth, stifling his urge to laugh. The driver's eyes flickered between the two of them for a second before settling firmly on the road. "Yes, sir."

"What were you thinking?" Danny demanded as the door to his apartment swung closed behind them. "Seriously, I know Don't Ask, Don't Tell got repealed, but I'm pretty sure that doesn't make it okay to feel me up in a cab."

Mike pressed close, hands on Danny's hips, probably as much to help him keep his balance as to get his hands on Danny. "You objecting?"

"Expressing concern," Danny corrected. "You want the guided tour?"

Mike groped Danny's half-hard cock through his jeans. "How about we start with this?"

"How about we start with the kitchen?" Danny countered. "Or maybe the guest room?"

"You're going to make me sleep in the guest room?" Mike let go of Danny, moving around to stand in front of him, so Danny had to fight to keep his face straight. "Weren't you the one talking about how good I look in my uniform?"

"Eh, that was before I had to deal with you and the obnoxious cabbie." Mike's face fell into exaggerated hurt, and Danny couldn't keep his game face on. Instead, he got his free hand on Mike's shoulder and leaned in to kiss him.

Mike deepened it, drew it out, hands carefully at his side—

there'd been more than one moment that had ended in the two of
them on the floor, back in high school, when Mike had touched
Danny in a way he wasn't balanced for. It felt good to kiss Mike,
good to kiss someone he knew and knew cared for him.

"How about now?" Mike asked quietly, drawing back.

"Now I'm thinking about how good you'll look out of that
uniform."

"And asleep in your bed?"

Danny shrugged. "As long as you don't snore."

"You know I don't."

"I do know that," Danny agreed. "So come on."

Mike hesitated partway down the hall toward Danny's room.
"You got a bathroom I can use quickly?"

"Gotta brush your teeth?"

Mike shrugged a little stiffly. "Thought I'd take a quick
shower. If you want."

Mike looked pretty damn clean, and he smelled amazing,
which could really only mean he was asking about one thing.
To which Danny was sure as hell not going to say no. "Through
there. Shower makes a weird noise sometimes, just hit it if it
doesn't stop."

"Aye, aye, sir." Mike dropped a mocking salute, already
turning the bathroom door handle with his other hand.

Danny collected Mike's duffel and stowed it in the corner
of his own room, fairly certain he'd made up the guest room
for no reason, then sat on the edge of the bed to take off his
shoes and socks. After a moment's hesitation, he stripped off
his T-shirt and pants as well, shoving the covers to the foot of
the bed. He lay back, arms behind his head, as he heard the
shower shut off.

The carpet muffled the sound of Mike's feet until he was
right outside the door. He stepped inside, his hair still damp,

wearing nothing but a towel around his waist. It was the first time Danny had seen him naked since college, and two years in the navy had been damn good to him: every muscle was toned, his tan going surprisingly far down. Apparently, sailors really did spend a lot of time walking around shirtless.

Danny let out a low whistle then, unable to resist, said, "Hello there, sailor."

"Really?"

"Really," Danny confirmed. "You want to get your ass over here, or you want to stay there and pose?"

Judging from how fast Mike was crawling over Danny, he wanted to get his ass over there, a sentiment that Danny could happily get behind. Mike was heavy, warm and a little damp against Danny's bare skin, his hands skating everywhere now that their ability to touch wasn't hampered by Danny's always-precarious balance.

Danny wasn't going to let Mike be the only one to take advantage of being horizontal. He dug one hand into Mike's hair, dragging him down into a kiss, all slick tongues and teasing nips. His other hand he traced down Mike's spine, dipping under the towel, working it loose. Mike moaned a little at the first brush of Danny's finger over the skin there.

"Feel good?" Danny asked.

Mike's hips flexed, making his hard-on obvious. "Really good. Like the first time, Danny..."

Danny's hand stilled as his heart tripped over itself. Mike's first time had been with him, and though they'd both had other partners in the intervening period, he had no idea if Mike had let anyone else do this to him.

Probably not the moment to ask, but he made a mental note to come back to the question.

For now, he was getting too caught up in the way Mike felt

on top of him to let much distract him. The towel finally came loose, letting him get his hand on Mike's ass. Mike's whole body shuddered as Danny brushed a fingertip awkwardly over his hole, dipping just the tip inside.

"Do it," Mike said against Danny's neck, adding a sharp brush of teeth that took care of getting Danny fully hard.

"Nightstand drawer. Lube and a condom."

"I can take it." Mike's hips flexed again, settling into a slight rocking that dragged his cock against the cloth of Danny's boxers, drawing the material over his own erection in a way that was almost painful.

"Lube," he said firmly, trying to keep his breath even. "It's sex, not endurance training."

"Could be both," Mike said, but he was already moving to retrieve the supplies, so Danny ignored that. Instead, he shifted as well as he could, managing to shove his boxers halfway down his thighs. Mike took care of them as he climbed back onto the bed, tossing them over his shoulder, probably in the same direction the towel had gone.

The way his muscles flexed as he straddled Danny made something in Danny twist with an envy that was never going to entirely go away. He wouldn't ever be able to do that, same way he'd never be able to go on his knees and suck a guy's cock, or kneel in the middle of the bed and take it. Not that he didn't have plenty of ways to compensate and work around, but sometimes he just wanted sex to be a little bit easier than it was.

"Hey." Mike must have read some of that on his face because the hand he used to cup Danny's cheek was gentle, rasping slightly against Danny's stubble, and his kiss was warm and affectionate. "Here, you insisted on using it, you can prep me."

He raised himself just enough for Danny to slide one lube-slick hand up his inner thigh, one finger slipping easily into him.

Danny forgot, then, about not being able to have sex exactly how he wanted to; he forgot about how Mike was only in town for a week; he forgot about everything but the way his fingers slid into Mike, the sight of Mike's cock, hard against his stomach, precome glistening on the head, and his own hand, pale against Mike's darker skin.

"That's enough," Mike said as Danny teased his entrance with a fourth finger. "Fuck, come on, do me already."

"So romantic," Danny teased, but he couldn't keep it up, not when his own cock was so hard he was afraid it might break off, his hands shaking as he reached for the condom. Smoothing it down his cock was an exercise in self-control when all he really wanted to do was give himself the half dozen strokes he knew it would take to get himself off. "You ready?"

"Been ready for the last ten minutes," Mike grumbled. He steadied himself with a hand on Danny's good hip, shifted forward a little. Danny closed his eyes, all the breath rushing out of him as Mike slowly lowered himself, tight and hot, onto Danny's cock.

When he was finally all the way down, they both moaned. Danny was sure he could feel the breath Mike took through his own body. "You feel so good," he said stupidly.

"You, too." Mike's eyes glittered, something more than amusement that was gone before Danny could pin it down.

Then Mike raised himself up and sank back down onto Danny's cock, and Danny let go of the thought. Let go of everything but the way Mike felt on his dick, the way his ass clenched around Danny as he shifted position to get Danny's cock on his prostate.

"You gonna—" Mike lowered himself again, voice cracking. "You gonna just lie there and make me do all the work?"

"Thinking about it." Danny nudged his hips up as much

as he could without knowing he'd be screaming in pain come morning. "I like you like this."

He did, but his hand was greedy for Mike's cock in it, the same way his own cock was greedy for an orgasm that wouldn't be long in coming. He took Mike in hand, rubbing his palm over the slick head to get some lube, then tightened his hand, stroking Mike in one long line that made his breath catch sharply.

"Do that again."

Danny obliged, matching the rhythm of Mike fucking himself on Danny's cock, losing himself in the sensations, the burn of his building orgasm in his muscles, his spine.

"Want to fuck you," Mike murmured. "Want to—your dick in my mouth, Danny, I want to suck you, I want you to suck me, want to fuck your face, your mouth, you've got the best mouth, Danny, I swear." He kept going, like a direct line to Danny's brain, the images building behind Danny's eyes as Mike spun out the fantasies in a voice that sounded exactly like sex.

It didn't take long for Mike's cock to twitch in Danny's hand, for his words to switch over. "I'm gonna, Danny, I'm close, I'm going to come, Danny, Danny, Danny..."

Danny felt Mike's ass clench around his cock, heard Mike's low groan as his orgasm started to hit him, and that was all it took for his own to crash over him, sharp and hot, leaving him panting and spent. Mike had collapsed on his chest at some point, only the head of Danny's cock still inside him, both of them breathing heavily and sweating.

"Fuck," Mike said, low.

"What you said," Danny agreed. He tilted his hips slightly, encouraging Mike to pull the rest of the way off, then took care of the condom.

Mike didn't move, his head resting on Danny's shoulder, his eyes closed. If past experience was anything to go by, he'd be out in the next five minutes. Danny wrapped his arms around Mike, pleased when Mike made a happy sound and snuggled further into him. The apartment would get cool when the sun started to set, but they had a couple of hours yet, so Danny didn't bother with the covers.

Instead, he ducked his head a little, pressing a kiss to Mike's forehead. "Welcome home, sailor."

MY FRIEND ZEKE

Martin Delacroix

Let me tell you about my best friend Zeke. And let me tell you what he did for me.

I've known I was queer since I was twelve. I never dated girls; their bodies didn't interest me. During high school, my sex life was a tube of jelly and my right hand. I kept my feelings a secret from everyone but Zeke. I didn't tell him until our senior year. My voice shook when I broke the news, but he handled my revelation with typical aplomb.

"You're gay?"

I nodded. "I know it's a shock, but—"

"*No problemo*, Andy. If I meet any cute guys, I'll send them your way."

That was Zeke for you: he didn't judge. Six foot three and sinewy, Zeke's rust-colored hair, riot of freckles and big smile disarmed people.

Everyone loved Zeke.

We roomed together at University of Florida. Zeke dated

a nice sorority girl, while I hooked up with guys through the Internet.

"Anytime you need privacy," Zeke told me, "just say so and I'll make myself scarce."

I took Zeke up on his offer, several times. But guys I met online were not looking for relationships. These were always one-time encounters—*wham-bam*—and nothing else. As my second year of college drew to a close, I felt lonely and terribly frustrated.

"I don't get it," Zeke told me when I explained my situation. "You're a nice guy, and good-looking, too." He ruffled my blond hair. "Most guys would *kill* for your dimples and blue eyes; the girls always talk about them when your name comes up. Face it, Andy: you need a *boyfriend*."

I bobbed my chin; I knew Zeke was right. I wanted a guy I could hold in my arms at night—badly—but where could I find one? I told Zeke, "I've tried two years now, without any luck. It's not as easy as you think."

Zeke shook his head and pointed a finger. "Maybe *I'll* find a guy for you."

I made a face. His remark sounded nonsensical.

Come on, I thought. *How would you do that?*

"Zeke," I said, "I don't know anything *about* sailing. Can't you find someone else?"

"There's no time. The boat has to leave Eleuthera within five days. Otherwise, my dad's stuck with Bahamian duty tax: six thousand dollars."

"I'd like to help, but—"

Zeke waved a dismissive hand. "I'll teach you everything you'll need to know. It's not hard, plus my cousin will be on board. We'll do four-hour shifts at the helm—a piece of cake.

Dad will pay us each five hundred dollars; he'll finance the food and beer, too. How can you say no?"

Zeke's dad owned a marina in Lauderdale. Once the boat was there, he'd refurbish it inside and out. Then he'd sell it for a profit.

"It's a forty-six-foot, ketch-rigged Morgan with a center cockpit," Zeke told me.

"A ketch *what?*"

Zeke rolled his eyes. "It has three sails."

He and I were home on summer break, with our sophomore year behind us. The economy was in deep recession, and temporary jobs for college kids were nonexistent. I flexed my fingers. The thought of sailing in open water frightened me, but...

Come on, chicken shit. Five hundred bucks with no taxes taken out? Do it.

I drew a breath and released it. "All right, Zeke. I'll go."

Our flight from West Palm Beach to Eleuthera took about an hour, but it seemed like five. I was scared shitless the entire trip. Our aircraft was a twin-engine prop model, with eight passengers and a pilot not much older than me. Every few minutes, the plane lurched up and down like an elevator out of control.

"We're hitting warm air pockets," Zeke said. "You're completely safe."

Keeping my eyes closed, I squeezed my armrests and prayed I wouldn't puke. Would the seasickness patch I'd stuck behind my ear actually work?

Thanks a lot, Zeke. This is just great...

Zeke behaved like he was sitting on his dad's Barcalounger back in Fort Lauderdale. His long limbs sprawled here and there. He yakked with other passengers like he'd known them all his life. Like I said: everyone loved Zeke.

From the air, Eleuthera looked like a crooked eyebrow. The airport in Governor's Harbour was nothing more than an asphalt strip and a one-story cinder-block building. Two customs officers checked our passports; then they pawed the contents of our bags before waving us through a pair of glass doors. Outside, in hot sunshine, a row of unmarked taxis waited for potential passengers. Drivers smoked or played cards on their trunk lids.

A grizzled black man missing most of his teeth drove us northward on Queens Highway, a two-lane road peppered with potholes. We encountered little traffic, just an occasional truck or car. The cab was a twenty-year-old Chevrolet station wagon with missing hubcaps, a cracked windshield and no air-conditioning. Warm air rushed through the car. I squirmed in the backseat while sweat trickled down my ribs. Up front, Zeke chattered with the driver like the two were old buddies.

I'd expected Eleuthera to look like pictures I'd seen of Bermuda and Nassau: pink hotels, traffic cops on pedestals, white sandy beaches and coconut palms. Instead, the island was hilly and sparsely populated. We passed a dairy farm, then a pineapple plantation. Forests of slash pines and Australian pines grew on both sides of the highway, groves of sea grape as well.

We crossed a narrow concrete bridge where a pass split Eleuthera in two. The driver stopped for a moment so we could study the divide. He called it "Glass Window." To our left, the turquoise Caribbean was as placid as bathwater. But on our right, the Atlantic frothed and pitched; its hue was close to cobalt. Waves struck craggy palisades, sending plumes of salt spray high in the air. A cool breeze swept through the taxi; it smelled fresh and briny. I looked up at the sagging headliner and drew a deep breath. For the first time since we'd left Florida, I felt myself relax.

Okay, Andy: maybe it'll be okay.

The plan was simple: Zeke, his cousin and I would sail the boat from Bottom Harbour, in north Eleuthera, to Fort Lauderdale—a four-day trip. Zeke's cousin was already aboard ship; he had stocked the larder and purchased alcohol. Our taxi left Queens Highway. The driver turned onto a narrow crushed-shell road bisecting a stand of Australian pines. The trees were so thick I couldn't see anything but needles and bark to either side of us. I felt like we were in a tunnel. The road was bumpy and our taxi pitched and squeaked. Again, my stomach felt queasy.

Please, god: let me stand on solid ground for ten minutes.

When we finally emerged from the pines, I squinted in the afternoon's brightness. A dozen sailboats bobbed in a calm body of turquoise water, protected from the Atlantic by a rocky island. The boats all looked the same—white fiberglass hulls, aluminum masts, sails shrouded in blue canvas—but only one had three sails.

I pointed. "Is that ours?"

Zeke nodded.

The taxi left us at a small marina with a concrete dock and diesel fuel pump. The proprietor had a beer gut, a ball cap and a scar like a centipede on his stubbly cheek. A British accent flavored his speech. Once we'd identified ourselves, he pointed to a fiberglass skiff tethered to the dock.

"Load up your gear, lads. I'll ferry you out."

The skiff's outboard engine chugged and sputtered as we crossed the harbor. The water's clarity amazed me; I saw an orange starfish twenty feet below the surface as clearly as if I held it my hand. The bottom was sandy and as white as table sugar.

"Unlike Florida," Zeke explained, "the Bahamas don't have rivers dumping silt into the ocean. The water's never cloudy here."

Up close, the Morgan was far bigger than I'd expected—you could've thrown a party for thirty on its deck—but the fiberglass hull was heavily oxidized. The canvas sail covers and cockpit enclosure were all sun-bleached; they bore numerous patches. The teak trim looked weathered and rust flecked the chrome brightwork.

Zeke clucked his tongue and shook his head.

"Dad'll have his hands full with this one."

A slender, dark-haired guy emerged from belowdecks. He looked the same age as me and Zeke and wore only board shorts. I saw dark hair in his armpits when he greeted us with a double-handed wave. After we boarded with our gear, Zeke made introductions while the man with the beer gut chugged away in his skiff.

"Andy, this is my cousin, Paul. Paul, this is my best friend, Andy."

We shook. Paul's eyes were emerald green, his brows thick and dark. His voice was deeper than mine or Zeke's. Stubble dusted his chin and cheeks, and his teeth looked like piano keys. When he smiled, it seemed as though someone had switched on a high-wattage lamp. Like me, he was half a head shorter than Zeke.

"Paul goes to Emory University," Zeke had told me during our flight. "He's a nice guy, and smart. You'll like him."

I surveyed Paul's lean torso, thinking, *How could I* not *like him?*

Paul pointed to an ice cooler. "You guys want a beer?"

Moments later, we sat in the cockpit, shaded by canvas. A light breeze cooled my brow while I sipped from a can of Beck's. Zeke and I had both shed our shirts, and I noted the difference between Zeke's beefy physique and Paul's slender frame. If Zeke was a bull, Paul was a gazelle. Zeke's calves were carpeted with

rust-colored fuzz, while Paul's were dusted with dark and delicate hairs; they reminded me of raindrops, cascading toward his
ankles. I stole a glance at his crotch. His cock bulged in one leg
of his board shorts and I felt a stirring in my groin.

Okay, Andy: behave. This cruise isn't about sex.

I shifted my gaze to the horizon while Zeke and Paul
conversed. Paul had flown down from Atlanta two days before,
connecting through Miami. He'd brought a cooler packed with
chicken, beef, pork and dry ice. "I've heard you can't buy decent
meat on this island." He'd bought the rest of our provisions in
Governor's Harbour: fresh fruit and vegetables, rice, pasta, and
beans, and plenty of beer and wine.

"We'll eat simply," Paul said, "but well. Nobody's going
hungry or thirsty on *this* voyage."

After we'd finished our beers, Paul led us belowdecks to stow
our gear. I'd never been on a sailboat before, and the Morgan's
roomy accommodations surprised me. Right away, I learned
nautical vocabulary. The boat's "beam"—its broadest point—
was nearly fifteen feet. A "master stateroom" with a queen-size
bed was "aft," i.e., at the rear of the boat. The "forward v-berth"
slept two persons on separate mattresses. The galley kitchen had
a double sink, propane stove and "twelve-volt" refrigerator. The
main "head" had a shower, tub, sink and toilet. Another "guest
head" was a half-bath. The dining area—or "mess"—had booth
seating for six. Storage cabinets and closets were plentiful, and
all the woodwork was lacquered teak.

Okay, the carpet was worn to the weft in places; the drapes
were faded. The upholstery bore multiple stains and looked
like something from my grandma's house. But our quarters
were spacious and bright nonetheless. Already I felt better
about making "the crossing," as Zeke had called it, to Fort
Lauderdale.

We drew straws, using uncooked spaghetti noodles, and I won the right to occupy the master stateroom. I stowed my gear there, then I fell onto the mattress, face-up. Fresh air entered through an open hatch above me. Folding my arms behind my neck, I watched fluffy clouds float across the azure sky while the boat rocked from side to side.

Not bad.

Paul stuck his head through my open doorway.

"Comfortable, Andy?"

I grinned and nodded.

Paul turned down one corner of his mouth. "'If you've survived Zeke's snoring two years, I guess I can handle it four nights."

I chuckled. *Poor Paul.*

Zeke's nighttime rumblings were legendary. In high school, a buddy had nicknamed him "Mr. Chain Saw" during a camping trip. When Zeke and I got to college, it took a month before I could sleep soundly in our dorm room, and *that* was using earplugs.

I spent the remainder of our first afternoon on the Morgan's deck, learning names of shipboard equipment: mainsheet, roller furl, winches and winch handles, running lights, and booms. I grew acquainted with the wheel, throttle and gear shift. Paul did most of the talking, and I found myself growing more charmed by him as each hour passed. I loved the sound of his voice and the way he gestured with his hands when he spoke. He was self-assured and purposeful, but friendly. I liked the way his wavy hair fell across his forehead and covered the tops of his ears.

Our dinner that night was baked chicken with rosemary leaves, wild rice and snow peas—all prepared by Paul. He served it with a jug of cheap chablis that burned the back of my throat on the first sip. Paul sat next to me in the mess; he smelled of soap and shampoo from his evening shower. During the meal, more than once, his knee touched mine. On each occasion, he left it there a while, and the first time this happened, I sprang a wicked boner. My hands trembled and my armpits moistened.

Ay-ay-ay, watch yourself, Andy.

Zeke and I did the dishes. Then all three of us sat on deck in the cockpit, passing the chablis jug between us and gabbing in the darkness. All around us, lights shone through ports on neighboring boats. A breeze blew; the air smelled fresh and clean. The Morgan rocked and our booms creaked while Paul spoke of Emory and his life in Atlanta.

"The school's tough—I study six hours a day—but I like it there. Atlanta has so much to do: clubs, professional sports, great restaurants. And Lake Lanier's a fun place to spend a warm day. Sometimes, a group of us will rent a pontoon boat and we'll party like fools."

Paul never mentioned girls or dating, as most guys would, and I thought, *Hmm, maybe he's...*

Then I thought, *No way. You're dreaming.*

That evening, well past midnight, I lay in my stateroom, bathed in moonlight. A breeze came through the ports. I was half-asleep when a knock sounded on my door.

"Andy, can I come in?"

Paul entered, wearing boxer shorts and nothing else. "I'm sorry," he said. "I know it's late, but I can't sleep for Zeke's snoring. It's driving me nuts."

My scalp prickled. *Go ahead, ask him...*

"You want to sleep in here? There's room for two."

"You don't mind?"

"Shit, no."

Paul closed the door. I scooted over and he climbed between

the sheets. I felt his body heat, smelled his skin and the tooth-paste he'd used earlier. Already, my cock was stiff. Paul joined his hands behind his head; he stared at the ceiling. His lips parted and moonlight reflected off his central incisors.

"This is *much* better," he said.

And I thought, *It sure is...*

Then I thought, *Come on, test the waters.*

I nudged Paul's knee with mine.

He nudged me back. Then he rubbed his calf against mine and our leg hairs commingled.

Okay...that wasn't subtle.

"Paul?"

"Yeah?"

"Did Zeke tell you I'm gay?"

He chuckled. "Why do you think I'm here?"

I shook my head. Then I chuckled, too.

Sex with Paul was better than good. I'd been to bed with eight or nine guys; some were okay, but nothing like this. Paul and I didn't just fuck, we made *love*. He kissed like a dream. Our tongues dueled like a pair of writhing snakes while our chin whiskers rasped. He licked my armpits, ran his hands through my hair, sucked my balls while squeezing my cock in his fist. I was slim like Paul and our whippet bodies worked in unison. Everything seemed to fit just right.

I wasn't a passive participant by any means. I explored every inch of Paul's wiry body, using my hands and tongue. I licked between his toes, pinched his nipples till he groaned. I nuzzled his pubic hair while I teased his erection. His cock was built like the rest of him: slender and pretty, with a strawberry-shaped glans. It leaked precum—little salty-tasting pearls I lapped up and swallowed with delight.

Of course, I'd never had sex on a boat before, and I liked

the way the Morgan rocked while we shared intimacies. Waves mumbled against the hull; they sounded romantic. There's something to be said for water's effect upon our five senses. It sharpens them, I think; I know it did mine. Paul's skin smelled like sawdust, his crotch like damp earth. His skin was smooth and warm, and his hair felt silky. The sound of his breath in my ear drove me crazy with lust. His big teeth looked beautiful in moonlight.

Paul suggested a bout of sixty-nine, and we got ourselves positioned. When he took my cock into his mouth, a shiver ran up my spine. I swallowed *his* cock and felt the swollen glans nudge the back of my throat. Then we both slurped away, applying pressure with our tongues and lips, pleasuring each other as only two guys can do. I took Paul's plump nuts into my mouth, one at a time, rolling them around on the surface of my tongue. I licked his taint, then his asshole.

Paul shuddered. "Got any lube, Andy?"

"In my bag. Why?"

He smooched the head of my cock. "I want you to fuck me with this big banana."

Holy crap...

At Paul's request, I took him doggie-style. When I entered him, he gasped. I felt his lungs pump, his hole flex.

"You okay?"

"Yeah, fine. Just give me a minute to relax."

I kept my cock inside Paul. His gut felt warm and *oh*-so-sexy.

"Okay," he said, moments later. "Fuck my ass."

I rocked my hips and Paul groaned. His hole flexed against the shaft of my cock, a love muscle caressing me. My hipbones slapped Paul's buttcheeks each time I thrust into him. We both sweated and our skin smacked every place our bodies made contact. Paul reached for the lube and squeezed some on his cock. Then he stroked himself while I kept thrusting.

"Jesus, Andy, this feels good."

He came first, spewing the sheets with his sticky load. He cried out, so loud I wondered if Zeke heard it at the other end of the boat. What would he say if he knew I was fucking his cousin?

Paul's lungs heaved while he caught his breath. I pulled my cock out of his hole. Then I jerked myself off, gripping Paul's shoulder with my free hand, feeling the taut muscle there. It didn't take long before my balls tingled and a shiver ran up my spine. I spewed Paul's back, a series of shots that made my body jerk.

Holy shit!

I'd never experienced such an orgasm; I felt overwhelmed. My vision blurred and my chest heaved. I collapsed onto Paul's back, and a mixture of sweat and semen glued us together. That may sound vulgar, but it wasn't. I felt we were one person instead of two.

"Andy, that was…*amazing*."

"It sure was."

Paul shifted his weight. "I want to do this again…if *you* do."

My pulse pounded in my temples. "I'd like that," I said, "but tell me something."

"What?"

"Does Zeke know you're gay?"

Paul moved his shoulders.

"I've never told him—not directly—but I think he's always suspected. Why?"

Next morning, Zeke was already above decks when we rose. He had brewed a pot of coffee; it simmered on the stove. Paul and I poured two mugs full. Then we both ascended, squinting at the sun's brightness.

Zeke sat in the cockpit; he studied a nautical chart. Sunlight reflected in his red hair. When he heard us, he raised his chin. His gaze met mine and he gave me an impish smile.

"You girls have fun last night?"

I looked at Paul and Paul looked at me. Our faces turned as red as ripe tomatoes, but we grinned just the same, in spite of the awkward moment.

I turned to Zeke and flipped him the bird while he cackled like an idiot.

Oh, Zeke, I thought, *everyone needs a friend like you.*

LANDLOCKED SQUID

Tanner

I'm so fucking out, man," Charlie sighed while tossing his hand on the table. My cock twitched as I looked at my tall redheaded shipmate. I'm hot and admit it—think smokin' Jonas brother with shiny black hair, matching eyes with lashes so thick they make every butterfly that sees them come and a body as ripped and taut as any in the fleet after months at sea.

But hot as I am, I knew I wouldn't be getting any closer to Charlie than the occasional glance at his brilliant red bush in the shower because the dude was straight as they come—besides, I'm not in the service to fuckin' date, it's my job. Of course, there are plenty of other gay service guys out there if I want to play, so why piss off the straight ones by hitting on them?

Besides, playing poker right then was my job, so I ripped my eyes off Charlie and put 'em back on my hand. I had nothing myself but wasn't letting anyone know. Our two other buddies were already out and at a nearby bar, so me and Charlie were the last two dudes from the ship in the game. I'm no poker player, as any of them could have testified. But shipmates stick together, especially on land and in the company of civilians.

There was a long pause before the one other player at the table silently lowered his cards to the felt and gave a slight nod to me. The pot was mine. Charlie grinned while I reached out and hooked the chips toward me.

I never won our games on board.

Ever.

Knowing it was time to go, Charlie and I left the table and joined Rich and Brinkley at the bar, where I of course paid for a few rounds. The only one missing from our little group of sailors in the sand in Las Vegas was Jacob, a tall, shy blond with sparkling green eyes and soft-looking lips who had begged out of the late-night poker game to get some sack time. I'd spent months mooning over the guy with that crooked smile and corn-silk yellow hair he kept cut high and nearly tight as a marine. While the rest of us showed random ink, I had the feeling that Jacob's skin was still a blank canvas; he was the kind of guy who kept up with modesty even in our cramped quarters.

I had never seen him naked in the shower (yeah, I'd kept an eye out for him lurking about with a towel, but no luck), and even on the hottest nights when we sat around in our skivvies shooting the shit, Jacob kept his T-shirt on. I'd never seen that broad chest bare, and yeah, I spent a lotta time trying to look up the leg hole of the (pristine!) breezy white boxers he wore. Hey, don't wanna piss anyone off by staring, but I'm not dead either! Jacob never smoked or drank (even soda!), and the closest he would come to cursing was the occasional "Man!" said with emphasis when he had done something wrong or was frustrated.

Probably his clean-cut choirboy look of innocence drew me, but it always seemed like there was some bad bubbling away just below the surface of the guy, and I wanted to explore that more than I wanted Ricky Martin to call me into his dressing room after a concert. And I wanted *that* pretty fucking bad...but not as much as I was hot for Jacob Miller.

I was just as glad he was not among the other dudes from our flight deck group right then because I was on beersky number threesky and I could focus on bullshitting with them—not that they weren't hot, I could just control my mouth around them and not have to work to keep from staring at Jacob. Or hitting on him or following him to the head and staring—y'know, the couple million things you can do or say wrong when you've had some oat soda. And no Jake for him, btw, he would correct with that sexy grin. Shit, even that worked my bead and all but made my dick hard.

It had taken all of us to convince Jacob to come to Las Vegas anyway. We knew he had strong religious beliefs but he never forced them on us—and that wasn't even his biggest beef with the trip to Sin City. If he was going to take leave time, even an extra day, he wanted to use it to go home. On top of that we had only been ashore for three days before heading to Vegas. The couple married guys had gotten some fun time in, but the rest of us didn't even have time to jack off on getting home. But we had bonded on the ten months out, a band of rowdy brothers who stuck together, and when Brink said he was going to take the marriage plunge and wanted us there, we all agreed that our version of the road trip was on.

Brinkley's family is one of those rare breed who lives in Vegas, so he arranged places for everyone to stay. Well, almost everyone. I had other plans while I was there. I'd just broken up with a guy before we shipped out and had kept my hands to myself (literally!) for the voyage even though I knew where the dark corners and hidden rooms were on the ship after three cruises. My heart was nearly mended and I was ready for some action, so I arranged a room of my own on the Strip so I could manage to get away to some of the gay spots during the wedding weekend. And was pleasantly surprised when Jacob asked if he could split the room with me rather than sleep at a stranger's.

Could he sleep in my room? Do ducks like to swim? Do dicks like to be sucked? Well, I'd managed to keep my hands to myself for a long time, so two nights sharing a room with Jacob shouldn't make me too insane, and private time with him would give me more jack-off material. Since I hoped to be going out to other rooms with other guys, the money saving would just be a bonus for the weekend.

Despite the other guys calling me a wussy for not taking my winnings to the high-end strip club they were heading off to, I hosted a last round as I made my good nights and then hurried out of the casino to grab a cab, barking out the name of a gay club as soon as I tumbled into the seat. I could feel my dick start to thicken in anticipation. I'd been surrounded by cock for months, seen lots of it in the shower and certainly made good use of mine but was ready to touch another one—to kiss, suck, touch one attached to another guy.

The gay dance club I had scoped out was packed, as I had hoped; by the time I had gotten through to the bar I had been hit on twice so knew my lucky streak was going to continue. And yeah, I know I'm hot and my haircut alone screams "military," which has guys comin' in their tighty whities. All that free time after duty is put to good use by some of us. Once you have watched every movie every guy has downloaded and played poker until you owe each other a billion dollars, the small, crowded gym becomes the hot spot on board.

I'm also a "hooker." No, not what you think, despite my brags about my looks. I work the cable to "catch" jets when they come in on the flight deck, often teaming up with Jacob on the other side. "Hookers" end up with huge muscles even if we don't lift in our free time.

Even the bartender winked when he slid the beer over the counter to me, "On the house," he said. "Wait for me by the door at last call and we'll go back to my place and you can fuck me raw, stud," is what he didn't say, but the way he briefly stroked his finger over mine as I wrapped my hand around the sweat-beaded bottle let me know that was how he felt.

My cock thickened to about half as I smiled back. Target locked and loaded. I was going to take a few laps and scope the rest of the prey and could always come back to finalize his nonverbal offer.

A Las Vegas gay bar on a hot Saturday night is a horny gay sailor's paradise. It wasn't raining men from all of the country, but the place was sure packed with writhing men of all ages and sizes, and many of them had opted to be shirtless despite the blasting air-conditioning. I was fully hard by the time I made my way through the crowd to the packed dance floor, where in minutes I had been pulled into the fray and managed to slip the T-shirt I was wearing up over my head between gulps of beer and was shaking my ass (okay, okay, my high hard tight ass...) with the rest of the group. I was something of a star attraction, if I say so myself. I also knew if a gay marine happened in, I would be tossed aside as if I were in full face drag.

So I made hay while the sun was shining, bouncing between a guy named Matt from Baltimore, a hot off-duty blackjack dealer whose name I never caught, two Johns, a Jason, a Kyle and, well, you get the idea—I was having a good time. I'd been dancing (and drinking and making out...) and wasn't settled on anyone in particular to leave the bar with (or go into the alley or to their car or a cab or even into a bathroom. Hey, I was young and horny, it happens) when I became the sailor meat in a couple sandwich.

Two hot guys about my age from Savannah? San Antonio? Salem? started grinding on me, and the next thing you know I was invited back to their hotel room. See? Wasn't going to have to worry about grabbing Jacob Miller in the middle of the night after all. I mean, who am I not to accept hospitality like that? We were already grooming each other like cats right there on the dance floor. Which I am not against, btw, but I *am* still enlisted, and while I am not concerned about asking or telling anymore, I am concerned about public displays of affection going too far, being caught on cell phones or other devices and getting back to my superiors, which could affect future promotions.

So I pulled the hand that had snaked down my (now unbuttoned) jeans and we made our way out of the club.

Now let me assure you I do *not* have the moral standards of Jacob Miller, or even a wharf rat (I'm a *sailor*, for fuck's sake!), but it did dawn on me as the guys and I slid into a cab and sent our arms crawling around each other like the tentacles of a (horny!) octopus that I had been in a relationship for a long time (I was young, a year *is* a long time...) before the voyage and was about to embark back on the sea of decadence with not one but two hot guys, guys who were in a relationship. *Some* information had been exchanged, and before even giving it much thought I hit them with "Um, you guys got lube 'n condoms?"

It was said much lower but it was heard, I could tell by the noncommittal muttering they both made.

As a couple they just hadn't really thought about those things for a while.

"S'cool, I got 'em." Hey, I was going to Las Vegas and hadn't had sex in over ten months, of course I was ready! "Drop me at my hotel on the Strip! I'll grab 'em and come to your hotel."

They offered to come to my room, but I said, "I got someone staying with me." A quick shower couldn't hurt for me, either.

There really was no need to explain anything, as we were still in the middle of our game of Admiral Perry in the Arc-Dick, meaning we went back to exploring each other's bodies as soon as I shut my trapsky. I also felt the beer I had been downing catch up to me—my bladder was sending an "I'm full" signal. Another reason to have a quiet, personal moment before our carnal carnival began.

We smiled all around and I left them to stride into the lobby like I owned the place. Surprisingly few people were around at that hour; I had the elevator to myself and hummed as I hurried down the long hallway to distract myself. I was also stroking the flat of my palm up and down over my crotch as my dick pumped both in sexual anticipation and in readiness for the head. By the time I swiped my keycard down the slot in the door, I was doing a happy little pee dance.

Throwing the door open and expecting darkness, I was mentally mapping out my path to the head when I suddenly found myself as part of *CSI Las Vegas*. No crime had been committed, but the room was certainly not as I expected it.

The television was the source of light, and standing in front of it at the end of the bed as naked as the day he was born was my temporary roommate/full-time shipmate Jacob Miller, hard cock standing straight up against the flat muscles of his stomach as he stared intently at the screen. He was so fixed on what he was watching that he did not immediately register I was there. My own need-to-pee situation halted for a split second as I took in the visual. In near slow motion I watched as Jacob let his head turn toward me, twisting that lean torso, cock following his head. I could not have been more surprised if I'd walked in on Ann Coulter making out with k.d. lang.

Holy fuck!

On board we all whacked it in the privacy of our own bunks—quarters were tight and you could usually tell when guys were at it by the overwhelming smell, but I had never imagined Jacob doing it. Oh, I had a lot of other scenes of him in my head, but this was way above my thoughts.

Then just like that the world snapped back into focus for both of us, and our eyes met just as my "Empty bladder now" signal started to roar again. Talk about that catch-22! *Do I stand and stare like a drooling fool at the hot guy I have been lusting after and piss my pants, or go take care of business?* I opted for the latter even though the former would have been so much more fun. As I dashed across the room I turned to grab another look (which was amazing, his muscular form lean and ripped) as he turned slightly back toward the television, then Jacob leaned down to make a grab for the comforter to try and cover his nakedness.

There was some kind of dark shadow on his chest and right shoulder, but I couldn't tell what they were despite staring at Jacob like I was an x-ray scanner. But my eye did catch the TV screen for a split second. Jacob Miller, blond, conservative, hot (and nicely hung, I'd just learned…) had not only been playing a porn, but it was a gay porn.

Unable to process all of that without wetting the rug, I literally made a leap of the last step into the bathroom, where I drained my half-stiff snake and washed up, rubbers, lube and hot couple forgotten as my cock fully thickened back up post piss at the thought of Jacob's naked body and hard cock. And that the movie making it hard was gay.

Taking a deep breath, I stepped back into the bedroom after scooping a strip of condoms and tube of lube from my shaving kit. There was no shame in my game. The television had been turned to another channel and Jacob's smooth muscular chest was again covered with one of those stark white T-shirts. He was sitting up in bed, hands around the remote instead of his hard cock, lower body covered by the bedding. The room was now lit by two sources, the soft glow of the television and the bright shade of red that had crept up Jacob's neck and flushed his face all the way to his ears.

"Hey, sorry, just had to get some stuff. On my way back out…" I trailed off as casually as I could.

"You won't tell anybody," the blond whispered, head hanging down.

"Dude," I said as casually as I could while dropping the sex tools I had in my hand to the nightstand on my side of the bed, "we all beat it. I was starting to think you were a robot!"

Jacob raised his head and gave me enough of a smile for me to know he was good, my cock twitching at his sexy grin.

"Yeah, but about the movie I was watching…"

"Yeah, about that. Why the fuck did you turn it off?"

"Well, I…"

"You do want to finish, right?" Okay, so I was leading and invasive, but what would *you* have done if you walked in and caught your wet dream going at it to a gay porn because he thought you were out tramping the night away in a strip club with your shipmates? Well there you go then, save the judgment.

I also knew that if the night was going to go where I wanted it to, I had to be careful and cautious.

When you offer a squirrel a peanut, you don't try to pet it. You don't chase a deer at a salt lick or, as I'd learned the hard way, disco dance at a trout stream. Luckily my pop had seen me do far more flamboyant things, so he just urged me to leave the river and go make mermen in the sand, which he knew I would be much better at than fishing. Not a stoop, my old man.

Leaning across the bed, I grabbed the remote and punched in codes until the movie restarted.

"No!" Jacob yelped in a horrified way as I pulled the image of two guys fucking back up onto the screen. "It's not just a dirty movie, it's guys!"

"I'm not Stevie Wonder." I smirked. Like smirking was going to help me get what I wanted, but my dick was already hard and I was all but ready to leap back to the other side of the bed and use Jacob as a landing strip. I'd show him some hooking like he'd never seen before!

"They're hot!"

"You like that kind of thing?"

There was a pause, long enough for me to know that Jacob was processing my response.

"Of course. A whole lotta guys like this stuff."

There was a moment of puzzled silence as Jacob let his eyes cut from me to the television and back.

I'd dropped the remote onto the pillow between us.

"Well, I gotta take off," I said, cock fully hard. At least I had a hot date lined up, but no matter how hot they were or what we did, I knew I'd be coming to the image burned into my brain of Jacob naked and jerking himself.

"You can stay." Jacob's voice had a tremble in it and there was a pause as he looked at me, this time with no blush, then sat up and crossed his arms over his chest and hooked the edge of the T-shirt up over the flat muscles of his stomach and on up over his head. He let the soft material drop to the floor next to his side of the bed and smiled at me. Jacob Miller may have fallen off the same hay truck I had, but the look he gave me told me I had way, way underestimated him.

"Wow! Nice ink!" I finally said, date forgotten as I slid down onto the bed after quickly unlacing and kicking out of my shoes and hoping to fuck I wasn't having some kind of 3-D wet dream. I peeled my sweaty tee up over my head and let it fall to the floor as well, forming a matched set of undergear on each side of the bed.

Jacob pulled the naked lower half of his body out from under the bedclothes, and while normally I would have been staring at his crotch, I was so taken with what I had thought to be dark spots on Jacob's chest and shoulder that I couldn't take my eyes off them. They were tattoos, a big one scrawled across his chest with the initials *RB* in the middle of it. The scroll/floral ink on his shoulder surrounded the name *Robby.*

Boldly reaching over, I traced my fingers over the initials, giving my sexy buddy a quizzical look.

"My kid...," he said, blush back in full form.

The mystery of keeping covered up was solved.

"Lives with his mom and I don't get to see him much." There was a story, a big good story involving innocent-looking Jacob as an unmarried father with his kid's friggin' name tattooed on him, but all it meant to me was *Game on!*

While debating which way to go, north to his lips or south to his throbbing dick, I paused, wanting to hear the story but knowing we'd need something to talk about afterward. But before I could make that decision the hot blond reached down; smoothing his fingers under my chin, he lifted my face to his and pulled me upward, bringing my lips to his.

Fuck!

Explosions! Rainbows! Rockets! All that crappy movie montage stuff, but I swear to Jupiter it was true and worked as he kissed me, his lips as soft and full as I always thought they would be. Falling fully onto the bed I slowly let my body slide against his, our bodies writhing together as we made out.

Jacob slipped a hand between us and wrapped his fingers

around my throbbing dick—made me so fucking hot I thought I would blow right there! Gritting my teeth, I held back, though, and let him pump me as we kissed. Breaking my mouth from his I skimmed my kiss-damp lips down over the length of his body, stopping at the quarter-size dark rings of his nipples. I ran my mouth back and forth between the two, licking and sucking on them as Jacob moaned and grunted, holding my head in place on each one until I broke free and continued to lick my way on down the length of his body until reaching the head of his thick shaft and licking it a few times to his moans before plunging my mouth down over the wide head.

"Oh fuck yeah!" Jacob sighed, pumping his hips up to shove his cock farther up into my throat as he splayed his hands over the back of my head. "Suck that cock!"

Hmm, with all this verbal it was pretty clear this was not the first sex rodeo Jacob had been in. While my mouth was still buried down over the full length of Jacob's shaft, ringed with his soft blond pubic hair, he slid wildly around, pumping and sinking his mouth down over my throbbing piece. Movie forgotten, we fell into the sixty-nine of all sixty-nines, both of us running our hands over each other's asses. Jacob sucked like a pro, easing his mouth up and down over my dick while squeezing my cheeks and pulling me in against him.

Moving my mouth free of his shaft I pulled us back against the bed, our heads falling onto the crumpled pillows in another long hot kiss. Jacob pushed his tongue deep into my mouth with me following suit as we slashed our mouth-slick dicks together, bodies clammy with sweat. Pulling my mouth from Jacob's, I swept a hand over his short hair, grinning down at him at the same time. Fuckin' wet dream come true...

"Wanna fuck? Saw some stuff in your kit." He grinned.

"Long as you do me, man." I smiled back, darting down for

a kiss before rolling off my buddy and grabbing the rubbers and lube from the bedside table.

I dabbed some of the clear jelly into one of the condoms, then slicked it down over Jacob's throbbing shaft, squeezing the wide head as he crossed his muscular arms behind his head. He smiled up at me as I swung a leg over his body and reached back to fit the wide head of his shaft up against the puckering hole of my ass and eased down onto it.

"*Fuck!*" he hissed, eyes closed as he reached up and grabbed my hips, holding me as I pushed down onto his dick. Falling forward I grabbed the pillow on the left and right of Jacob's head as he lifted his muscular thighs and pulled me up against his body, holding me tight up against himself while pounding his thick cock up into me. I started to move my arms just as Jacob moved his, wrapping them around my back to pull me down against him, our mouths pressing together, tongues slowly going in and out between our lips while his dick slid deep into my asshole. Time seemed to stand still as he moved in and out of me.

Pushing myself back onto the bed, I rolled Jacob over on top of me, his cock never leaving my hole as he continued fucking me, my arms wrapped around his back, and held him tight. We continued kissing until Jacob finally broke our mouths apart and lifted me higher until he was pile-driving his dick into me. Long, ragged streaks of his sweat tracked down over his body and rained down on me, my hard cock pushed up into the flat muscles of my stomach as he braced himself on my legs.

"Gonna go, man, here it comes," Jacob moaned while slamming himself into me. I could feel the throb of his dick in the tight, slick muscles of my ass. "Yeah, man, gonna go..."

"Come on me," I groaned as he stroked in and out. I grabbed the base of Jacob's dick and held it in a circle of fingers until I felt him begin to blow, his cock throbbing sexily against my fingers as I slowly skinned the rubber up over the end of his cock until only the tip was pushing in and out. When he began to yelp I yanked the rubber off and squeezed the head until he shot, face scrunched up in concentration. I held his dick until his hot come slashed out over me, covering my cock with his thick white-hot slime.

"Oh yeah, fuckin shoot, man!" I encouraged, *"Fuckin yeah..."*

As I was covered with hot, slick come I grabbed my own cock and gave a few strokes, shooting my own hot load over my body. Jacob collapsed onto the bed next to me, panting choppily. We lay quietly for a moment, sweat and come dripping down over the side of my stomach, after the most amazing s-e-x I'd ever had!

"That was fun. Gotta smoke in that bag of tricks of yours?" innocent Jacob Miller turned his head and asked.

"Man, how deep *is* that quiet well of you?"

Shrugging, he traced a broad finger through the pool of come on my stomach and smiled, his high beam that I could have seen through the filtered light of the porn (gay porn...) playing on the television opposite the bed.

"Let's get high and talk about it."

Fuck. It was going to be a long hot weekend, and I doubted that we'd even leave the room, blowing off the wedding just like I'd blown off the couple.

But it would be so worth our buddies' anger, I thought as my cock started to get hard again and I rolled off the bed to get the smokes, both kinds, out of my shaving kit.

LET US GO DOWN TO THE SEA

Michael Bracken

I worked behind the bar at McGinty's, pouring drafts and opening bottles for hardworking men fresh off the boats and for tourists seeking authentic dockside experiences. The place had been in continuous operation since the late 1800s, with modern conveniences such as electricity, indoor plumbing and pressurized beer dispensers added over the years. The years had been good to me as well, but though I'd matured from delicate to wiry, I remained too short to look most men in the eye.

There were a few rooms on the second floor, but the only one still furnished was a one-room efficiency where Peg-Leg Pete had lived before his daughters moved him to a nursing home. When one of our regulars had too much to drink, I would walk him upstairs to Pete's room and let him sleep it off. Sometimes I even crashed there myself, remembering the nights when we were young that I had spent in Pete's arms.

At the front of the building, over the entrance to the bar, Pete's room faced the harbor, and anyone standing at the window could watch the fishing boats leave each morning and return each evening. Pete had often done just that, and he never failed to keep me apprised of the comings and goings of all the vessels in the harbor, from the working craft for which it was their home port to the pleasure craft that occasionally visited. We often joked that Pete was waiting for his ship to come in, but little did I know that he wouldn't be watching the harbor when it did.

The Veterans Administration would probably have helped Pete obtain a prosthetic limb, but he would have none of it and pshawed anyone who made the suggestion. His wooden leg, the eye patch he sometimes wore over his left eye and sometimes wore over his right, his grizzled mug with its permanent three-day growth of gray stubble, and his oft-told tale of losing the bottom half of his left leg to a great white shark that rivaled anything Peter Benchley ever created had tourists lining up to buy his beer. The fact that he could see perfectly well out of both eyes and that he'd actually lost his leg when it caught in a cable being drawn in by a purse-line winch while working on an American seiner in 1951 didn't slow him down any. His tale of battling the shark just grew as the years passed.

I missed Pete after his daughters had him taken to the home, and I visited when I could. I sat with him, held his hand and shared whatever dockside gossip I had heard in the bar that week. I didn't know if he heard me or even knew I was there, but it comforted me to know that he might. He had been the only man I ever loved in a community where one could never express that love in public.

Afterward, I would return to my home, uphill and six blocks inland from McGinty's, open a Sam Adams and sit in the living room staring at the harbor and the Atlantic Ocean beyond, remembering those carefree days before the navy took Pete away to search for Nazi U-boats, when we spent days in his skiff, skinny-dipping in a secluded cove we discovered and cooking fresh-caught fish over open fires on the beach. After the war, Pete did what every red-blooded American boy did back then: married and produced a new generation of Americans. His marriage was over long before he lost his leg, but he and his wife kept up appearances for years, she turning a blind eye to my relationship with Pete.

When his youngest daughter graduated from high school, Pete left his wife and took a room on the second floor of McGinty's, where I had been working—first as a busboy and later as a bartender—ever since my 4-F status prevented me from joining Pete on the front lines.

I often cadged two beers from the cooler and carried them upstairs to Pete's room. Some nights we would just sit and drink and talk and stare out at the harbor. Other nights we were more physical, and we made love until the wee hours of the morning when I had to slip out and return to my own home before the town awoke.

Late one fall afternoon, a few months after Pete had moved out, I saw a thirty-five-foot Beneteau First 35 motoring into the harbor, its sail down and a burly, dark-haired man at the wheel. I was headed in to work and I paused on the cobblestone street outside McGinty's to watch the sailboat dock and its lone occupant disembark. Somehow, I knew I would see him again later that day.

Had Pete still been around, he would have known everything there was to know about the stranger, and he would have shared that information with me before the man walked into McGinty's late that night and straddled the stool at the end of the bar under the neon Sam Adams sign, the same stool Pete had preferred during his days of beer drinking and tale spinning.

The stranger's black hair hung in ringlets to his broad shoulders and his beard brushed his thick chest whenever he moved his head. His skin, what was visible of it through the tattoo sleeves and the mask of hair, had been tanned the color of aged leather. He ordered dark rum, and the tumbler in which I served it disappeared when he wrapped one meaty fist around the glass. Business was slow, with only locals occupying the place until the stranger's arrival, so I tried to engage him in conversation between orders. When I asked his name, he said, "People call me the Captain."

I said, "I've not seen you here before."

"I don't usually sail this far north."

"So where you from?"

"It's not where I'm from that's important," the captain said, "it's where I'm going."

I bit. "So, where are you going?"

He smiled through his beard. "We're all going the same place, John," he said, "eventually."

I replaced his empty tumbler with a fresh one and moved down the bar to wait on two brothers who were busy trying to drink each other under the table. Not until sometime later did I realize I hadn't told the captain my name and, unlike bartenders at hotels and chain restaurants, wasn't required to wear any form of name badge. I puzzled on that while I poured beer, freshened bar snacks and swapped gossip with the sea-salted fishermen who found McGinty's a dark, wood-paneled purgatory between the hell of their homes and the heaven of the open sea.

When I finally returned to his end of the bar, the captain had finished his second tumbler of rum and was ready for a third. As I slid it across the worn wood of the bar, I asked, "Do we know each other from somewhere?"

"We've never met," he said, "but I know you."

Before I could follow up, one of the drunken brothers slapped the other end of the bar, startling me and causing me to turn.

"What're you mumbling about down there, old man?" he said. "Get us another round."

I moved down the bar. "You've had enough already," I suggested.

"Not if my brother's still standing," he insisted. "He doesn't have his beer legs yet."

After I glanced at my watch, I relented and opened two more bottles of Sam Adams. The brothers wouldn't have much longer to drink, and I knew if they didn't fall in the harbor as they wobbled down the dock, they could sleep it off on their boat.

The captain sat at the bar the rest of the night, nursing his rum and watching me work. No one approached him and no one spoke to him but me. He still occupied Pete's stool at last call and was still there at closing time a few minutes later after all the other patrons had been shooed out. I cashed out, switched off all but the night-lights, poured the last of the captain's rum in a clear plastic to-go cup and escorted him to the exit.

When I opened the door to the street I found Pete reaching for the knob. He wore cheap cotton pajamas with the nursing home logo printed over the left breast and he appeared clear-eyed and freshly shaven for the first time in more than a year. He stood in the open doorway, grabbed my head between his hands and held it while he planted his lips on mine, right there in front of the captain. When he finally pulled his face back, Pete said, "I've missed you."

"I've missed you, too," I told him.

The captain said, "I'll wait."

Then he stepped past us and sat on the curb, his plastic cup of dark rum still gripped in one meaty fist.

After Pete entered the bar, I locked the door behind him. He took my hand and led me up the steps to the room that had been his. Once inside, he pushed me back against the door and kissed me again. His kiss was deep, penetrating, breath-stealing, and it filled me with the same desire and quivering anticipation that our assignations after skinny-dipping in the cove had all those years earlier, when our bodies had been young and hard and we were still searching for ourselves.

He unbuttoned my shirt, pulled it free of my chinos, and pushed it off my shoulders. My undershirt followed, then my shoes, socks, chinos and BVDs. His pajamas joined my clothing on the floor and, as our clothes fell away, so did our wrinkles and the ravages of aging. Perhaps it was just memories of better times clouding my vision, but I saw the young man I had fallen in love with rising naked from the water in our secluded cove, stepping off the Greyhound bus fresh from the war in his navy dress whites, disembarking from one of the American seiners in his plaid wool shirt and jeans after a long day at sea.

His broad shoulders and thick chest tapered down to a flat stomach and narrow waist held aloft by powerful legs, and the mast that was his cock rose from the wild tangle of dark hair at his crotch without need of chemical assistance or manual manipulation, just as it had when we were young and still navigating the uncharted waters between lust and love.

As I dropped to my knees before Pete, I wrapped one hand around the thick shaft of his cock, surprised and delighted at how firm it felt in my fist. Several times I slid my fist up and down Pete's tumescent cock before I leaned forward and wrapped my lips around the spongy soft head. A bead of precum oozed out of the tip and I licked it away.

I slid my lips down Pete's mast, taking ever more of his cock into my mouth until I had to move my hand out of the way so that I could take it all in. Then I drew back until my teeth caught on his glans. I did it again and again, and each time I took his entire length into my mouth, the dark tangle of Pete's pubic hair tickled my nose and his heavy balls bounced against my chin like a pair of boat fenders.

I wrapped my arms around his powerful thighs, caught his asscheeks in my hands, and felt them tighten and relax as he began moving his hips forward and back, meeting my oral caresses with increasing vigor. When his ball sac began to tighten and he wrapped his thick fingers in my hair, I knew he wouldn't last much longer.

And he didn't. With one final thrust, he came, sending wave after wave of salty sperm splashing against the back of my throat. I swallowed and swallowed again, and when Pete's cock finally stopped spasming in my mouth, I pulled away and looked up at him.

He took my hand and helped me to my feet. Then he turned me around, and he stood behind me as we faced the window and looked across the harbor. Two dozen American seiners were lined up at the dock awaiting the crews that would take them to sea early the next morning, and I could see the captain's sailboat moored at the far end of the dock.

Pete leaned over my shoulder and whispered into my ear the same things he'd told me when we were younger, about how we'd been made for each other, how our love would allow us to overcome all obstacles, how we were as good as married even if no one else knew. "Look out there," he whispered as he pointed to the Atlantic Ocean beyond the entrance to the harbor. "What do you see?"

"Endless opportunity," I whispered in return, a call and

response from our youth when our entire lives were ahead of us and not behind us.

He kissed my shoulder and the base of my neck. One arm wrapped around me and his strong fingers trailed down my chest, down my abdomen, to my erect cock. He wrapped his hand around it, nearly engulfing it in his big fist. As he continued kissing my neck and shoulder, he stroked my cock and I leaned back against him, comfortable in his arms. I had never had Pete's stamina and I came quickly, sending a thin stream of cum shooting toward but not quite reaching the window.

By then Pete's mast had risen again and I could feel his cock snuggling between my asscheeks. He stepped away and returned a moment later with a partial tube of lube, last used several months before he was taken to the nursing home. He uncapped it, coated his middle two fingers and then slipped them down the length of my asscrack to my porthole of pleasure.

I bent forward and he massaged my sphincter until he could slip one finger into me. He continued his digital manipulation until he could also slip in his second finger. Then he withdrew them both, pressed his cock head against my lube-slickened hole and pushed forward.

When he was deep inside me, just as he had been so many times in the past, every memory of our lovemaking flooded through my mind, from the first time as young men after skinny-dipping in the cove to the last time in Pete's room as old men barely able to coerce our cocks to attention. But what I remembered most were the good times, the best times, the times when we were young and could experience orgasm after orgasm as if they would have no end.

As I relived those memories, Pete stood behind me, holding my hips as if at the helm of a personal pleasure craft, and he steered us toward paradise, drawing back and pushing forward, moving slowly as if we had calm seas ahead of us forever.

But we didn't. He began moving faster, harder, driving into me, pounding into me, the rough seas of sex lashing against us, my own cock swelling again so that I had to take it in my hand, matching my rhythm to his as I jerked my mast, and I came and Pete came and he released inside me and he held me until his cock stopped spasming and he could finally pull away.

We collapsed on his old bed and looked at each other, seeing what had been and not what was, and we held each other, feeling what had been and not what was, and we talked about what had been and not what was. For those few hours that one night we were young again, and we were whole again, but when it was over we were old men again.

"I have to go now," Pete finally said. "The sea is calling."

He climbed from the bed and opened the closet, where some of his clothes remained because I could never find it within myself to discard them. He dressed carefully.

"Take me with you," I asked from the bed as he reached for the door.

Pete turned and said, "This trip's not for you."

He left me alone in his old room over the bar and clumped down the stairs.

I pushed myself off the bed and stepped to the window, where I watched the captain rise from the curb and take Pete's arm. Together they crossed the street and headed down the dock. The sound of Pete's wooden leg clicking against the cobblestones echoed through the still night air, replaced by the sound of his leg thumping against the weathered wood of the dock.

The captain helped Pete into his boat. Then he cast off and the Beneteau First 35 motored away from the dock. Once clear of the harbor, the mainsail rose, and I watched Pete and the captain sail into the rising sun.

I returned home before the town awoke and the dock filled with fishermen preparing for the day, and I didn't need to answer the ringing phone that greeted me when I pushed the door open to know that one of Pete's daughters was calling to tell me that Pete's ship had finally come for him.

ANGEL

Bearmuffin

I was in New York City, shooting photos for an S/M article I was going to write, when *Raunch* magazine's travel editor offered me a tempting assignment. He wanted me to do a piece on Turkish oil wrestling. There was a tournament next month in Edirne and he wanted me to go, all expenses paid.

It was the perfect job for me. I love hunky Mediterranean men, the handsome brutes! Their dark, exotic eroticism thrills me to the core. I could easily imagine sweaty, dark Turkish hunks, their bulging muscles dripping with olive oil, stripped to the waist in leather britches, grappling in the summer heat. It gave me the biggest erection of my life just to think about it. Of course I accepted and began making travel arrangements. My plan was to take some great pictures, do some hot and heavy cruising, and maybe even come back with a husband!

I booked passage on the *Ulysses*, a Greek freighter bound for Istanbul. I preferred traveling on cargo ships and freighters because the passengers were usually older, more intellectual types mixed with offbeat, artistic types. Life aboard a freighter is more exciting but quite mellow and I would be able to get some writing done without being disturbed.

I find that traveling on freighters gives me the opportunity to meet some interesting people, providing some intriguing grist for my literary mill. Once in a while I would meet some really hot and trippy guy. We'd have a little affair on board for the time it took to get my destination. I still kept in contact with a few of these guys, who lived all over the world. When occasion permitted I would see them again and fuck. But I didn't know anyone in Istanbul, so this time out I would have to make new friends.

I stood on the docks, smoked a cigarette, and watched the hunky dock workers loading cargo containers onto the ship. I couldn't keep my eyes off them, for they looked so sturdy, so strong, so muscular. The testosterone-fueled spectacle inflamed my lusts and I found myself sporting a hard-on, which I promptly tried to hide when the first mate came up to greet me. He showed me to my cabin, which I was pleasantly surprised to find was quite comfortable, spacious and clean.

The first mate told me the *Ulysses* had six officers and twelve crew aboard. In addition to me, there were three other passengers. "I would appreciate it if you didn't interfere with the crew when they are at work but you are free to go about the ship," he said. I wasn't quite sure what he meant by *interfere*. Did he spot my gay vibe? Was it his way of saying the men were off-limits? Whatever.

The first mate gave me the meal times. And I had a choice. I could dine with the officers or the crew. You know me, I chose the crew. Since it was close to dinner, he expected me to join them in the mess hall in a few hours. Now, that was something to look forward to. With all those horny Greek sailors, there's no telling what mischief I might get into.

I found the mess on the main deck. The room was big enough to accommodate three four-place tables, which had been placed together for the crew and any passengers who might choose to dine with them. I made a quick survey of the room and sat down at the table with the hunkiest and handsomest of sailors. I was to be the only passenger to dine with them, the other three passengers preferring to dine with the officers.

Some of the crew spoke English, which I didn't think unusual since I figured they often had contact with English-speaking passengers. One of the sailors, a shaggy-haired stud with a handsome face and a lean, sinewy build, asked me where I was from and other personal questions. I didn't mind answering because I think sharing experience is all a part of travel. Then another member of the crew commented on the fact that I didn't have a wedding ring, so he asked me if I had a girlfriend.

I was about to say that I was gay but one of the older men at the next table blurted out, "Girls? Girls? Let him fuck girls. But not marry them. Marriage. Bah! I've been married three times. It was a full catastrophe!"

I had to suppress my laughter because he was right out of a favorite movie of mine, *Zorba the Greek*. He broke out with a broad, all-knowing smile. The rest of the men laughed. Well, he seemed so sincere that it seemed a shame to burst his bubble, so I just nodded and smiled.

I noticed that most of them sported wedding rings. My instincts told me that it would be best to be discreet with these men. I wasn't quite sure how much they approved or disapproved of homosexuality, but they assumed I was on the make for chicks. If anybody was interested in any kind of homosexual hanky-panky, they would reveal themselves. I didn't speak a word of Greek, but the international language of love would easily take care of that obstacle.

We were lucky the ship had a great chef, for the food was hearty and simple Greek fare but delicious and filling. My favorites were the dolmades (stuffed vine leaves), lamb kabobs and the moussaka, which is a sort of Greek lasagna made of eggplant, potato, cheese and ground beef topped with a creamy béchamel sauce and baked to perfection.

Bottles of ouzo were passed around and we all washed down the excellent Greek cuisine with the strong liquor, which tasted like black licorice. It sounds sort of gross but actually was quite good.

I drank some more ouzo and told the crew some of my travel stories, making sure to include some made-up tales of wild sex, which they especially appreciated. I was in the middle of a story when this Greek youth walked in and sat down in front of me. I was immediately taken by his beauty. I figured him to be in his early twenties with a lean, muscular physique and an alluring but commanding presence. I got an instant hard-on. I wondered if he could see the lust in my eyes.

I had a hard time concentrating on my story, and to this day I don't remember what I was saying. His eyes were mesmerizing; he looked right into me, and I felt my pulse quicken. All I was conscious of was this stud who looked like a Greek god come to life. I had fallen under his spell. I dared not look at him for fear of losing control and doing something I'd regret. For I wanted to go to him, embrace him. I'd hold him in my arms and nuzzle my face in his hair, behind his ears and neck and then kiss him, fervently, passionately while I felt up his impressive muscles. Fortunately, somehow I was able to restrain myself.

I heard some of the men call him "Angel" and that's exactly what he was. An angel of almost ethereal manly beauty. The

Ancient Greeks believed that the gods produced offspring with mortals. Angel could have been the son of Adonis and some beautiful water nymph. He had a neatly trimmed beard and a mustache that framed his sensuously curved lips. Lips that begged to be kissed. Kissed by me! And I would kiss the rest of him: pecs, abs and his ass.

I fantasized about his cock. Yeah, I'd get his big Greek cock totally hard. I'd roll the foreskin back over his cockhead, stroke the rock-hard shaft, watching the foreskin slide back and forth over the head until he squirted a salty load of hot cum all over my face.

I was so fucking horny that I knew I'd come in a flash if I didn't restrain myself. All he had to do was stick his hard cock up my ass, give my hot ass a good pumping and I'd shoot hot loads of cum all the way from here to Pittsburgh.

I noticed he glanced at me a few times, once smiled, but didn't seem interested. And how could I blame him? Here I was passing myself off as straight, and right in front of me was the most desirable man I'd ever seen. Oh well. As Elizabeth Taylor once said: "You can't always fry the fish you want to fry."

After dinner I walked on deck for some exercise. But I was feeling a bit tipsy from all that ouzo, so I decided to turn in early. I had a couple of gay novels I had purchased in New York. Those and a bottle of good Russian vodka would be my company for the night.

I started reading my novel but I couldn't help but stroke my cock a few times as erotic images of the young Greek studs I had met at dinner fueled my homoerotic fantasies. Angel, the divine Angel especially, was in my thoughts. I imagined doing the nasty with that hot Greek stud. I opened the vodka and had a few doubles. Still I couldn't sleep, so I went on deck to check out the action.

On deck some off-duty sailors were smoking and talking. The night was warm but crisp. The ocean calm. A warm breeze caressed my face and the salty sea air was invigorating. I had a sense of freedom being on the freighter; the power of the wide open spaces made me think of destiny and fortune. "O Fortuna" from Carl Orff's *Carmina Burana* kept going through my mind.

My initial reaction was to join them and strike up a conversation, but I had second thoughts about that. Perhaps they were discussing their job, or even talking about loved ones they'd left behind, a girlfriend or wife perhaps. I felt I'd be a third wheel. And I found myself feeling a bit lonely, wishing that I had someone special to think about back home.

I banished these sad thoughts and fished out my cell phone and started looking at some pictures I had taken back in London of me and this hot stud having sex. Rimming, fucking and sucking. The basics. Once again, I became quickly aroused and my cock began to stiffen in my jeans.

I suddenly heard a friendly *hello* behind me. I turned around to see Angel looking at me with a curious expression on his face, interest tinged with excitement. I gazed upon his face for a moment and was struck by his natural masculine beauty. His hair was curly and black, his eyes also black. The face was angular and open. His jaw was strong, his teeth perfectly white. His hands were thrust into the pockets of his uniform, which fitted him tightly and emphasized his robust physique. He truly had a body to tempt the very gods themselves.

Well, the potent combination of vodka and ouzo had me quite tipsy. "Wanna see something?" I handed him the phone. He took it and began looking at the pictures one by one. Then he stopped. He was particularly interested in two of them, for he kept flipping back and forth between them. I looked at them and grinned. He was flipping between the ones of me sucking cock and getting fucked.

He looked at me and smiled lewdly. "Is that you?"

"Yeah." I grinned. "See something you like?"

He laughed and nudged me with his elbow. Then he reached down and grabbed his crotch.

"You want to do this?" he said, showing me one of the ass-fuck pix with my heels in the hair and the stud ramming hard into me. "You want to fuck?"

"You bet!" I said.

He spoke in a plangent baritone, his accent British. It intrigued me. "Your stories," he said. "About fucking women. I did not believe you. I had a feeling about you. That you were gay."

Thank god Angel's gaydar was fully operational. I was somewhat embarrassed by the ruse and blushed, but Angel took it as a big joke and laughed good-naturedly.

"Yes, I am gay," I said. I was reckless. I leaned toward him and kissed him. "God, I want you so bad!"

"Careful," Angel said, lowering his voice. He hesitated for a moment and looked around to see if anybody was watching us. The deck was deserted. He kissed me gently and patted my ass. Even then I had the impression that he was relaxed, totally at ease and happy to be in my company.

He explained to me that he had to get back because his cabin mate was an older guy who was nosy and always kept an eye on him and was forever asking him questions. It turned out to be the one I called Zorba, who had commented so emphatically about fucking girls. Angel added that I was right to pretend I was straight. Though they were good men, the crew was not especially open to homosexuality; some of them were downright hostile to anyone who was gay. "We will meet tomorrow night. Midnight."

"Come to my room. It's below the first deck. Room 24A. But what about Zorba?"

"Don't worry. I know what to do."

"Your name. I don't know your name."

"Angelos," he replied. "Call me Angel."

"Angel, I really like you."

"I like you!"

And with that he kissed me and slipped away into the darkness.

Angel must have struck some deep chord within me, some kind of pagan yearning, for I found myself thinking of Ganymede, who was kidnapped by Jupiter to be his lover. I looked up into the star-filled sky and began to intone words of a strange impromptu prayer in which I invoked the ancient Greek gods of homosexuality: Apollo, Dionysus and Hermes Pan, to smooth the way for me and Angel to enjoy each other's company.

The next morning I wrote in my journal and then finished reading one of my gay novels. The writing was shamelessly erotic, which only served to arouse me further, making me think about Angel and all the fun we would have together that evening. Whatever he was planning to make our tryst possible, I prayed fervently that it would all work out.

Later that day I ran into my fellow passengers, a retired physics professor and his wife, a former ballerina with the New York City Ballet. A bit before my time, I'm afraid, but she and he were charming. They seemed interested in my work and asked me questions. I did my best to satisfy their curiosity. The other passenger was a tall, lithe and sort of '70s woman who was going to Istanbul to buy antiques for her shop in Greenwich Village.

I had my meals with the crew as usual. Angel was there but he remained discreet and only smiled at me from time to time, as nonchalant as if we had never met. I realized that it was necessary to maintain discretion if we were to commence our affair. As for me, I was consumed by an impatient lust to be with him. My cock was hard and I felt drops of precum stain my jeans, but somehow I was able to continue my charade of being a big stud with the ladies and told the crew more stories. By the time dinnertime rolled around I was horny as hell and the minutes crawled by like hours, so anxious was I to be in Angel's company.

At midnight there was a knock at my door. It was Angel who couldn't wait to rush into my arms. We began kissing hard and passionately, our hands roaming hotly over each other's bodies. We kissed for a few minutes and then got out of our clothes. We were that impatient to explore each other.

I paused to admire Angel's slender but powerful physique. He was an Adonis who very much resembled Michelangelo's famous statue of David. He had the same sloping muscles, the powerful upward curve of the buttocks, the same perfectly formed biceps and pecs. His abs were hard and furrowed. His cock large and uncut, curving downward over his impressively large balls. He was a living work of art to me.

Angel responded to my adoration with equal ardor by paying me one compliment after another. "I love your blond hair, your hazel eyes," he said, brushing a hand over a shock of hair that grazed my forehead. "You are so handsome." Then he squeezed my biceps. "You have strong arms." Suddenly, his hands went for my ass. I could feel his powerful hands kneading my buttocks. "Tight ass," he said. "I love that, too!" I couldn't stop blushing but was so happy to see that I appealed to him.

I asked him if he would let me take his picture. He agreed and after a few initial shy poses he posed for me like a muscleman and flexed his muscles. "I could do a porn movie," he said playfully.

"Oh yes, you could," I said emphatically as I took more pictures.

I sniffed the air and I could smell him, his natural manly smell mixed with a spicy aftershave, and the whole effect was very erotic. I wanted to lick his ass, run my tongue all over his body.

Of course, I went right for Angel's meaty pecs. I rubbed Angel's nipples between my fingers, pulling and tugging ever so gently. I flicked the edge of my fingernails over the tender tips, making the young Greek Adonis gasp with pleasure.

I was so fucking horny. My puckers twitched at the thought of Angel ass-fucking me. My cock bolted over and over, so eager was I to have him fuck me. I took out some lube from a bag and rubbed it all over my asshole. Angel grinned broadly as I did this and started to run a hand over his cock, getting it good and hard for me.

I lay on the bed and thrust my legs into the air. Angel immediately responded to my invitation and positioned himself between my legs. I could feel the blunt head of his cock brush against my spasming puckers and I let out a cry of anticipation and yearning. And yet I had to restrain myself and not be too loud a moaner because no telling who my cabin neighbors were.

He ran his hands over my asscheeks, slowly and deliberately, and then moved a hand into the cleft of my ass, where he inserted a finger in the crack and slowly ran it back and forth, deeper and deeper, until he had reached my anal puckers. He brushed the tip of his finger along the hole and circled it, immediately eliciting a gasp of pleasure, which encouraged him to begin inserting the finger deep into my hole.

Angel knew how to work on an ass. He massaged my back and buttocks, kissed and caressed my thighs and asscheeks. He spread my cheeks and blew his warm breath over my hole.

Then he nibbled around my taint, the sensitive area between the cock and the asshole. He got everything really warm, wet and lubricated with his saliva. When he licked gently and tapped his tongue gently against my hole, I sighed deeply as waves of pleasure engulfed me.

"Ah, ah, deeper, deeper into my hole," I said, wishing it were his cock inside me. He soon granted my wish and once again applied the head of his cock against my hole. He reached over and began lightly playing with my nipples as his cock began its descent into my ass canal.

He was halfway up my ass when I gave out a stifled cry. God, he was so big!

"Are you okay?" he asked.

"Yeah, I am. Give me a moment to relax. You got such a big cock and I'm so tight. Let me relax a minute." I fished into my sex kit for a bottle of poppers and took a good whiff. I offered some to Angel but he declined.

Instead Angel took out some Moroccan hash, put some in his little silver pipe and shared it with me. "Open your mouth," he said. I did as he asked and he blew the sweet smoke into my mouth. I inhaled deeply and within a half a minute, my hole begin to relax and my mind went into a dreamy haze as my whole body relaxed and his cock continued its way up my hole until it hit my prostate.

I moaned again.

Angel paused for a moment to allow his mighty cock to plump up inside me.

"I love my cock inside you."

I was impatient for him to begin fucking me. "Fuck me, Angel. Fuck me hard!"

"You like it rough?"

"Yeah. Fuck me good and hard."

And with that encouragement he proceeded to do just that. Our bodies moved in unison to the rhythmic pumping and thrusting of pelvis against butt, his cock pumping in and out of my ass. I had to remind myself not to cry out too loudly, but he was a powerhouse fucker and that was hard to do.

I was high as a kite on the hash and the poppers. The potent combo relaxed my body and my asshole so that I was able to let his wonderful cock glide past my sphincter.

I propped my calves on Angel's broad shoulders and he pulled me to him. From time to time I kissed his sensuous lips and he whispered Greek words for *ass*, *fuck* and *cum* into my ear.

Hot streams of sweat streaked down our bodies and we were having the fuck of our lives. I sensed that Angel was ready to come, and so I squeezed my asshole muscles around his cock, milking it for all it was worth. He tossed his head back and cried out, "Ah fuck," and slammed into me and held his cock steady inside me as it exploded and the hot cum spurted out and seared my hot asshole. He pulled out and I looked into his eyes and began jacking off my hard cock as he played once more with my nipples, getting me good and hot until I unleashed my own hot load, which landed in thick, hot spurts all over his well-muscled abs.

Afterward, we drank some more ouzo and just lay in each other's arms, gazing into each other's eyes, our souls filled with the promise of love and complete perfect brotherhood.

A sudden thought occurred to me. I asked him what he'd done about Zorba, his cabin mate.

He chuckled and ran a finger along my chin. "I bought him a bottle of ouzo. He loves to drink. We talked and talked until he got drunk and passed out."

Angel's resourcefulness in the face of adversity made me swell with pride. I kissed him on the lips.

"So we have all night?"

"All morning!"

We spent the rest of the morning getting to know each other better. Between bouts of hard, sweaty fucking, sucking and rimming, we told each other our stories and came to an understanding.

He was born in Athens but migrated to England, where his dad opened a Greek food store. That explained his British accent. After some years, his family returned to Athens and retired. He was twenty and decided to become a sailor and work on freighter and other cargo ships. He'd been working on the *Ulysses* for five years.

He sat propped up on the bed with his hands behind his head. I could see the perspiration glistening in his bushy armpits, streaking his chest. He was smiling down at me. My face was resting on his half-tumescent cock and balls. I could smell the hot sweat wafting from his pubes and bushy armpits. It was a light musk, the kind of manly fragrance that never failed to arouse me.

As I lay between his muscular legs I ran my hands all over them, feeling the sweaty muscles glide under my palms, finally going up toward his crotch and playing with his cock and balls. I looked up at him, my eyes filled with desire. He returned my gaze with one equally horny. So I ran my hand up and down the thick shaft, pulling back his foreskin to reveal an especially wide cockhead. I noticed a drop of precum glistening in the peehole and he got harder, so I knew he was fully aroused. I sucked his cock once again and within minutes he came to a full climax, filling my mouth with his salty Greek sperm.

We smoked some more hash and he told me he worked in the engine department assisting the engineers in maintaining the equipment in the engine room.

I asked him if he enjoyed being at sea. He said it was okay, but he did not seem particularly enthusiastic, though he mentioned the pay was good compared to what he could get home back in Greece. $1,500 was a lot of money back home. His mom and dad depended on that income.

"Do they know you are gay?"

"I don't think so. But I would not tell them. I don't think they would like it."

I felt very sympathetic to his plight. It was clear that although he was making good money, he did not have the freedom to be himself either on board the freighter or with his family. I promised myself that if I were ever in a position to change that, I would. And as I ran my fingers through his curly black hair, I thought how different it would all be if he could live a free and open gay life.

"If there's anything I can ever do to help you, Angel, let me know. Okay?"

He smiled and kissed me. "I will," he said.

I kissed him back. "I mean it."

Angel kissed his forefinger and traced my lips with it. "I know." His gentle gesture warmed my heart. I couldn't help but fall in love with him.

By the time we docked in Istanbul, Angel had purchased at least fifty dollars' worth of ouzo to keep his cabin mate well out of our business. I somehow knew that Angel would be more than just another fuck buddy, that my affair with Angel was something more serious, more profound. I had high hopes of a life with Angel forever by my side.

Angel and I had one last night of uncontrollable passion before I had to disembark and head for Edirne, where the wrestling championships were to be held. There were plenty of hot, hunky wrestlers, but none could compare to my beloved Angel, and all through that week I did nothing but think and fantasize about him.

That was a year ago. Now Angel is here with me in San Diego. He's just come back from playing soccer. He's all sweaty and I love it. I adore his smell, his scent, his musk. It makes me so horny.

You can see that I kept my promise to help him. When he said that he wanted to come live with me I was able to get a visa for him through my friends at the State Department.

I made him my photographer's assistant and so he was able to help out his family. His brother and sister-in-law moved in with his parents to take care of things on the home front. Once Angel and I get married, it should be no trouble to process a permanent visa and eventually get him naturalized as a United States citizen.

Whenever I'm in Angel's arms, and that is quite often, I often think of that starry, balmy night on the *Ulysses*. I remember my fervent prayer to the Greek gods. To this day I thank them for our happiness.

BOOTS FOR THE GODDESS

Connor Wright

Wind wept around the eaves and windows of the shrine, giving the normally peaceful room an unsettlingly sinister mien. Kelvi rose to his feet, kissed the marble cheek of the goddess's statue, then stepped aside to let the woman behind him make her own petition. He opened the door just as lightning blazed across the sky; its attendant thunder drowned the tolling of the watch-bell.

Pulling down his hat, Kelvi snorted. Everyone in town knew damn well a storm had come—the bell was a little superfluous. At least with the racket going on he could work as late as he wanted without complaints from his neighbors. Kelvi made his way back to his smithy, his prayer running through his head the whole time.

The watch-bell was ringing again. Kelvi dropped his tongs—and the shutter-latch they held—into the quenching bucket and walked out into the street.

"What is it?" The baker's wife was squinting toward the bell tower.

"No idea," Kelvi said, shading his eyes and turning away from the tower, looking out toward the sea. Perhaps... "I'm going down toward the harbor."

"Do you really think—"

"Tevseth doesn't *believe* in drowning," Kelvi said, and set off at a trot. The memory of his husband making that declaration years ago had been one of two gossamer filaments of hope to which he'd clung over the last two and a half weeks.

Kelvi's features were like those of most others in town: gold-brown hair, skin burnished bronze by sun and wind—though perhaps not quite as dark as some; his most unusual feature was green eyes where most had brown. He hadn't shaved in a while, and he never could be bothered to comb his hair, as it made no difference in its appearance. His husband Tevseth, though, was an entire head taller than Kelvi; broad shoulders and brawny legs well-suited to helping haul in nets full of fish; his skin nut brown and his hair closer to auburn, thanks to far more time exposed to the elements.

Exclamations and shouts went up from the seaward side of town, urging him onward. At the top of the harbor's ramp, a knot of people were pointing, waving, weeping: a ship was coming in.

The *Sea Dragon* was sitting low in the water, low enough that even Kelvi could see that something was wrong. He could tell something was amiss with the sails, as well; there weren't enough of them and those that remained seemed to be the wrong shape for where they were rigged. Men moved across the deck, which looked normal enough, at least until they'd maneuvered into the slip.

Kelvi, half a head shorter than most of his neighbors, elbowed his way to the front of the crowd. As a result, he and the town's healers were the first to see the true damage sustained by the crew. Every one of them sported bandages, even the captain, who led a procession of two pairs of men, each carrying a shrouded body.

"Tev," Kelvi said as Tevseth joined the captain. His husband's left arm was bandaged; dark circles smudged the skin under his eyes. Outside of that, he was still the man Kelvi knew. "Are you—"

"It's only a scratch," Tevseth said, his expression still troubled. "It's not important. Kelvi… We, uh, we lost two men. Kiseth and…" He closed his eyes and turned his head away, jaw tight for the long moment of silence. "Hathvit."

"Hathvit." Guilty relief, which had taken root the moment Tevseth had crossed the deck, was joined by hollow disbelief. How could they—he, the *Sea Dragon*, the town as a whole, their friends and neighbors—have lost two young men? Hathvit was Kelvi's own apprentice and a new father.

"Step aside, please." Letha, one of the town's healers, repaid his earlier impatience by bumping him out of the way with her hip.

When Tevseth finally, awkwardly, climbed down, Kelvi drew him away from the rest of the crowd. "You're sure you don't need to see Letha?"

"It's only a scratch, I promise," Tevseth said, pulling him into an embrace. "I just want to go home."

"As do I." Kelvi gave him a squeeze, then stepped back, took his hand and led him up the ramp toward their snug house.

On their doorstep, Tevseth paused again to cup Kelvi's face and tilt his head back before he leaned down and kissed him. "Missed your voice, Kelpling. Missed your face and everything about you." He would mourn later. Now, home again, with Kelvi warm and alive under his hands, he would thank the goddess for reuniting them.

Kelvi kissed him back, running his fingers through Tevseth's hair. "I know. I was… When I thought…the worst, I was always grateful I'd gotten up to say good-bye."

"Told you," Tevseth said, ducking his head so he could nuzzle the skin just under Kelvi's ear, "told you I don't *believe* in drowning. Waste of time." Underneath the usual words, though, was his own gratitude that they'd been able to say their good-byes.

Kelvi laughed and fumbled at the latch, closing his eyes as Tevseth lifted him over the threshold. "I know."

"I was glad, too. And… The knife you made me, it probably saved us all." Tevseth pressed his forehead to Kelvi's as their hands met on the hilt of the knife at his hip. "I had to come back to tell you."

Instead of saying anything, Kelvi tilted his head and kissed the bigger man, kissed him as hard and as deeply as he could.

"Mmm," Tevseth said, opening to his lover and clutching at Kelvi's shirt. "Bed now," he gasped when Kelvi pulled away for a moment, then shoved his shirt up to put his hands on bare skin.

"*Bath* now. Love you dearly, but you're—" Kelvi groaned as Tevseth simultaneously pinched his nipples and sucked at the side of his throat. "Tev, you've been at sea for almost a *month*."

"If you love me—"

"Hush," Kelvi said, putting his fingers over the bigger man's mouth. "I'll wash your back."

"Oh, all right," Tevseth said, his tongue flicking out around Kelvi's fingers. His husband's skin tasted smoky, metallic; tasted of Kelvi's forge and honest labor.

"Good. Now." Kelvi drew his hand away and caught both of Tevseth's, mindful of the bandage on his left arm.

They made it as far as the door to their bathing room, where Kelvi halted and pulled Tev down to claim another kiss.

He kissed back, losing himself in the heat and the sweetness of the embrace. Tevseth's hands found Kelvi's shirt, pulling it free of his pants, the man himself reluctantly drawing back so he could lift the garment over Kelvi's head.

"Piecemeal won't work," Kelvi said, shifting a half step backward so he could open his own trousers. "Naked now, Fishy."

Kelpling and Fishy, silly pet names that sent a happy ache twisting around his heart and throat. Tevseth fumbled at the laces of his own boots, finally getting them undone, then skinned out of his clothes once they were off. When Kelvi was undressed, he held out his arms.

"You smell," Kelvi said, stepping into Tevseth's offered hug anyway, "but I *have* you to smell. That—"

"I know," Tevseth said, bending his knees and getting his hands under Kelvi's legs, then hitching him up so he could carry him into the bathing room. Despite Kelvi's relatively small size, he was heavy with muscles earned through long hours at his anvil; despite Tevseth's determination to put his sorrow aside, it was too new not to bite. "I know, I know, and I have you, too. Even if I couldn't help, even if I couldn't keep Hathvit safe for you. For his family."

"It's all right." Kelvi put a hand on Tevseth's right cheek, pressing his own to Tevseth's left, at the name of his apprentice. "I know, *She* knows, that you would have, if you could. It's not your fault, and please, please, don't—" He kissed Tevseth, kissed a line from cheek to mouth and then pressed his forehead to Tevseth's. "Tev, Fishy... Put me down?"

"But..." He let Kelvi slip from his hands, holding him steady until he stood on his own.

"Hush." Kelvi put his fingers to Tevseth's lips once again, then let them fall away as he pushed up to give him a brief kiss. "You get the water started, I'll find towels."

Tevseth nodded, turning away from Kelvi; he kept glancing at him as the other man moved across the room. While Kelvi looked over the shelves where they kept the towels, soap and other bathing necessities, Tevseth turned his attention to the tub. It was sunk into the floor, lined with slick-glazed tiles, with a tap jutting out over the edge closest to the wall. He pressed the wide stopper into the drain hole at the bottom, then opened the valve to fill it. A cistern on the roof, painted black, held and warmed the water; gravity led it to the tub.

Kelvi put the towels he carried on a small stool that stood beside the tub, then put the soap dish, a wooden cup, a sponge and two slim bottles down on the floor below it. He held Tevseth's hand as they watched the water level rise, then leaned over and turned off the tap when it reached the halfway mark.

The water was warmer than the tiles, but cooler than his own skin. Tevseth didn't mind, carefully kneeling in the bottom of the tub and watching Kelvi step in as well.

They passed the cup, sponge and soap back and forth as they washed each other, punctuating the slow process with quick kisses along arms and shoulders and collarbones; lingering kisses when their mouths met.

"Tilt your head back, Fishy." Kelvi reached for one of the two bottles.

"Clean water first," Tevseth murmured, and opened the drain. The level of the murky water dropped, slowly at first, then seeming to move more quickly as the draw of the drain grew obvious.

"I... Sometimes, I...worry. About you, and the boat, sailing into something like this," Kelvi said, trailing a finger through the edge of the miniature maelstrom the drain created.

"I've never seen one," Tevseth said, pushing his hand through the center of it. "Not one large enough to sail into. Mostly we worry about rocks." He looked up, into Kelvi's eyes, his hand rising to catch the other man's chin and hold him still. "All I wanted was you. To come home to you." With that, he leaned forward and covered Kelvi's mouth with his own, his tongue sweeping over Kelvi's lips before slipping between them.

He met Tevseth's kiss with a sound of want, opening his mouth and abandoning the bottle he held in favor of resting his hands on Tevseth's biceps.

"Now," Tevseth said, putting his hands under Kelvi's backside and pulling him up so their stiffening cocks nestled beside one another, "will you have me? Now?"

"Yes," Kelvi said, clutching at broad shoulders, rolling his hips as skin slid against skin. "Yes, yes, *yes*."

A breath and then Tevseth rose, dripping; he kissed Kelvi thoroughly before he began to edge toward the side of the tub. He carried the smaller man carefully across the floor to the bench that stood near the shelves of towels and other supplies, relaxing his grip only once he'd straddled the bench and sat down.

Kelvi straightened up and pulled down the nearest towel, then set to work drying them off. He worked from their feet upward; a kiss to the head of Tevseth's cock, followed by a little lick, and he was gone again.

"Kelpling," Tevseth said, as his husband dropped the towel, "need to *touch* you."

"Just let me—there," Kelvi said, taking another bottle from the shelf and offering it to him. Turning around, he put one foot over the bench and leaned over, supporting himself with his hands.

Tevseth put the bottle down and watched as Kelvi moved, putting his hands on Kelvi's ass and spreading him wide as the man bent over. He kissed and licked his way from Kelvi's perineum to the small of his back, then down again to linger in the spot that made him squirm.

"Ah! Oh, you're *teasing* and I thought you needed to touch me." Kelvi shifted his weight, slowly, his breath hitching as the tip of Tevseth's tongue flicked delicately across his skin.

"'M touching you," Tevseth said, with a squeeze. "Love you clean like this." He sat up a little and nibbled his way along the curves of Kelvi's buttocks.

"Tev, Fishy, that's—oh…" Another, somewhat faster, shift as Tevseth held him wide again and licked at puckered flesh. "Give me more? *Yes.*" He hissed the word as Tevseth's tongue pushed into him.

There was only so much teasing Tevseth could stand, and he was the one providing it. One last lick and he straightened up, looking for the bottle, locating it by his foot. "Still for me?"

"Don't make me wait." Kelvi let his head fall forward, reaching back to hold his erection and his bollocks to one side. He could only see part of the other man, a slice of his abdomen and a flash of the head of his cock. Tevseth's finger, slick with oil, pressed against him and he did his best to relax and let it in.

The room was not quite silent, their breathing loud in their ears; Kelvi's pleased sound when Tevseth's finger found his sweet spot echoed off the tiles.

"Don't, don't, *don't* tease, Tev, *please*—" Kelvi moaned some minutes later. Tevseth's fingers curled, thumb rubbing at the skin just behind his bollocks and the two inside him riding the sensitive organ; his knuckles went white and his nails dug into the wood of the bench. "Take me! Please, by the goddess, Tev…"

"You want me?" Tevseth said, his voice oddly gentle.

Kelvi turned around, setting one knee on the bench. It was his turn to cup Tevseth's face, to tilt his head back, a rare enough occurrence that he took the time to savor it before kissing his husband. "Yes," he breathed, afterward, "yes, take me, now."

"Just a moment." Tevseth poured more oil into his hand, on the careless side of generous, then set the bottle out of harm's way. Once he'd leaned against the wall, settled a little lower on the bench and slicked his cock, he put his hands on Kelvi's hips and tugged him closer. "Come here."

It was awkward, at first, straddling Tevseth and holding himself up. Kelvi didn't mind, though, busy kissing and being kissed while Tevseth guided the head of his cock between Kelvi's buttocks. He reached down and adjusted the position of it, then lowered himself a little. "Ah!"

"Won't hurt you," Tevseth said, his eyes closed and his jaw tight as he clenched his teeth. "Won't move till you say."

"Fishy-love," Kelvi whispered into Tevseth's ear, then licked-sucked-bit the lobe, "*Take* me."

"You want—"

"Fuck me, take me, mark me, make me yours all over again, do it fucking *now*, please—*Yes!*" Kelvi let his head fall back as Tevseth thrust up into him.

He turned his head and pressed his lips to the tender skin at the base of Kelvi's throat, then bit down, sucked hard. Kelvi squirmed in his lap and he made another mark on the other side, pushing up again as the man shoved himself down.

"Tev, lover mine—Yes—" Kelvi dug his nails into Tevseth's shoulders, rocking, making needy, desperate noises at the back of his throat.

"Come?" Tevseth could feel Kelvi's cock rubbing against

him, leaving little smears of wetness behind, the man's body squeezing his own erection.

"No," he panted, then stilled and kissed Tevseth, smiling against the man's lips as Tevseth whined.

"Come," Tevseth said, doing his best to make it demanding. Kelvi had risen off him a little and he could clearly feel every trick his lover used to reduce him to nearly wordless need. "Kelp*ling*—"

Kelvi dropped into Tevseth's lap once more with a small gasp. "Need to hear *you*, Fishy-love."

"Oh." He found Kelvi's nipples and rolled them, hunched over so he could bite and suck at another bit of unmarked skin.

"Just fuck me," Kelvi murmured, wriggling under his touch, sliding his hands over Tevseth's back.

"Yes," Tevseth grunted, thrusting into him, closing his eyes as Kelvi rose and fell in concert. He ran his hands over Kelvi's sides, his thighs, his back, needing the reassurance of the contact and wanting to reassure through it.

"There," Kelvi breathed, combing his fingers through Tevseth's hair, kissing him without regard to where his lips landed. "Now, Tev, come for me?"

"Mmm." Tevseth panted as he fucked the other man, fingers tightening on Kelvi's thighs as he did. His climax started with his toes curling and a stillness that echoed the wood beneath them as exquisite fire flashed through him. A low, shuddery moan escaped, half-muffled by the crook of Kelvi's neck; Tevseth's grip dug deep enough to leave accidental bruises that he would kiss, guiltily, later.

"You're *home*, Tev," Kelvi whispered, petting Tevseth's hair, his own eyes closed. "You're home, and I've got you."

"I am," he said, smoothing his hands over Kelvi's legs before working his right hand between them. "I know." Tevseth started with gentle strokes, his head resting on Kelvi's shoulder, nose not quite pressed against the side of Kelvi's neck.

"More," Kelvi said, kissing the side of Tevseth's face, "please—yes."

Tevseth tightened his hand around Kelvi, whispering, "Your turn."

Kelvi leaned back, propping himself up by holding on to the bench and letting his head drop. The change in angle drove little high-pitched sounds out of him as he moved, as Tevseth's hand and softening prick worked the oldest magic of all on him.

He let Kelvi set his own pace, one hand squeezing the shaft of Kelvi's cock while the other stroked hard and fast over the head of it, foreskin and slickness making it easy.

"Pretty Kelpling," Tevseth said, smiling as Kelvi's usual annoyance was replaced by a wordless cry, Kelvi's body bucking and jerking under his hands. When the other man relaxed, Tevseth lifted his hand to his mouth to lick and suck his fingers clean; Kelvi shoved himself upright and kissed Tevseth around them—Tevseth's cock twitched at the feeling and he wished not for the first time that they were sixteen all over again.

"So good to have you home," Kelvi said, softly, "it's not the same without you."

Kelvi's curiosity got the better of him as they headed into town. "What happened?"

"It was... It was... It was just water. Hathvit and I, we were going to go up to cut down one of the sails because it was torn and was going to break off the top of the mast. We were the... the best choice. We had lines tied around us, tied to the rails... Before we could get up, out of the way, a wave...a wave came over the rail. And he slipped, and I couldn't get to him."

"An accident."

"I should have—"

"An *accident*. Tev, don't—"

"I couldn't—I couldn't help him. Hathvit was...he was your apprentice and I couldn't—" Tevseth's voice hitched.

Tevseth's gentle heart was one of the things that had drawn Kelvi to him; one of the things he most prized in his lover. He held fast as Tev mourned for the both of them.

"I'm sorry," Tevseth said, a bit later, sniffing and finding his handkerchief.

"For what?" Kelvi kissed his shoulder, then spoke without lifting his head. "I *know* you, Tev, and I know you wouldn't have let *anyone* get hurt if you could. Hathvit and everyone on the Sea Dragon knows. *She* knows. None of us blame you."

"I know, but it still doesn't..." Tevseth gave a great shuddering sigh and shook his head. "I'm home, and Hathvit..."

"His family won't blame you, either. We'll help them, Tev. I promise."

"All right. Good." A deep, shuddering breath and he pulled himself up straight.

Kelvi gave him a wry smile. "You know, if I had told him no, if I'd forbidden him to go out fishing—"

"But it's not your fault—Oh," Tevseth said, blinking at Kelvi.

"You're not the only one feeling responsible, Fishy." Kelvi linked his arm through Tevseth's and tilted his head toward the street. "Let's go see the rest of our family."

"All right." Tevseth looked down as they entered the market square, his attention caught by something strange in Kelvi's appearance. "Kelvi, those are your old boots."

"Yes," Kelvi said, glancing at his feet.

"Why? You just bought new ones." He watched the cracked

leather folding as Kelvi moved; could see Kelvi's toes through the holes.

"Because I needed you to come home, so I gave my new ones to the goddess." The memory of them sinking out of sight flickered across his mind's eye and he squeezed Tevseth's forearm.

"Kelvi, Kelpling, you..." Shaking his head, Tevseth marveled at his life. This was the man he'd married, who sacrificed something he needed for *him*.

"I'll get a new pair. Tethiva's shop survived all right," Kelvi said, gesturing across the square at the cobbler's home. "If I'd thought of it, I'd have added my favorite hammer and asked for Hathvit and Kiseth, too. You're all irreplaceable, but things are just...*things*. Come on."

And so they went, to halve sorrows and double joys, to mourn together and be grateful together.

HEAT
LIGHTNING

Neil Plakcy

W hat do you mean you can't go with me?" I asked. "We've had this transport on the books for a month. And we're scheduled to leave tomorrow."

"Got a better offer, dude." Rob was a pierced, tattooed twenty-something who danced at a gay club in Wilton Manors for tips. But he had grown up on Nantucket and knew how to handle any kind of boat, so I hired him when he was available to help me move boats around Florida, the Caribbean, and the southeastern U.S. But this was the second time he'd flaked out on me, and I was over him, even if he was cute.

"Where am I going to find someone to replace you?" I groused.

"Try craigslist. There are all kinds of crazy ads online there." Then he hung up, leaving me crewless.

I've built a list of recreational sailors I can call on for part-time work—bartenders, substitute teachers, the able retired and so on. They have to be knowledgeable enough about boats to be trusted with a pricey yacht, as well as available for irregular work on short notice.

I spent the next hour on the phone but came up with nothing. The trip up the Intracoastal to Hilton Head was going to take most of a week, and no one else could swing the scheduling. I was willing to try anything at that point, so I put together a quick ad for craigslist. *Wanted: experienced sailor to assist with yacht transport from Ft. Lauderdale to Hilton Head. Salary plus return transport.* I added the dates we'd be gone and my email address and chose the *help wanted* column. Just for grins, I also posted it under *men seeking men.*

I was irritated about the short notice, and also about losing the benefits that came with sailing with Rob—watching his handsome tanned body at work, cranking sails or polishing teak wearing nothing more than a pair of deck shoes and a smile. And every once in a while, when he was horny and could forget that I was twenty-plus years older than he was, we had amazing, mind-blowing sex.

It's hard to be a single fifty-something gay man; you're invisible in a bar until you open up your wallet and start stuffing bills into a dancer's thong or buying drinks for a twink who's always looking over your shoulder to see who else is coming in. I've tried dating guys my own age, but the ones who aren't already partnered are usually single for a reason, either physical or emotional. Not that I'm picky, but I draw the line at morbidly obese, suicidally depressed and chronically unemployed.

I was about to give up and call the client to reschedule or cancel when my computer pinged to announce a new email. It was from an address I didn't recognize, FLguy52, and the subject line read *craigslist ad.*

My heart skipped a beat. Was it someone looking for sex? Or a guy who could sail? At that point, I was hoping it was a sailor.

Eddie wrote that he'd been sailing since he was a kid and had owned his own boat back in New Jersey. He was available when I needed him, but wanted to know more about the job. He ended with his cell phone number, and I called him immediately.

We talked for a couple of minutes, then made plans to meet later that evening for coffee at the Panera Bread on Federal Highway in Fort Lauderdale. "How will I recognize you?" he asked.

I was about to say that if he was under thirty he'd probably look right through me, but instead I said, "Fifty-four, dark hair and glasses. I'll be wearing a baby blue polo shirt with *Brooks Yacht Transport* on it."

"Baby blue," he said. "I can find that."

I picked him out as soon as he walked in the place. His dark hair was salted with gray and slicked back, showing off a receding hairline. He wore a Tiffany rubber choker with a titanium clasp, a Tommy Bahama Hawaiian shirt and white shorts. His face was round and friendly, and he was, like me, about twenty pounds over his optimum weight. But his skin was a ruddy tan, a good sign among sailors.

"I'm Phil Brooks," I said, standing up and sticking out my hand.

"Eddie Kanter," he said. "With a *K*."

We both got coffee and sat at a table by the window. "The boat's a sixty-four-foot Offshore Voyager—a sportfisher. You know it?"

He shook his head. "Mostly stuck to sailboats. The biggest I've ever had was a thirty-two-foot Pearson with a fifteen horse-power engine. But I've been on every kind of boat you can imagine, helped out with sails, tiller, even a little engine maintenance."

"You still have a boat?" I asked.

"When I got divorced, my wife got the house, the kids and the IRAs, as well as my left testicle. I sold the Pearson when I moved down here."

That settled it. He'd seen the ad under the *help wanted* section. Too bad. "What kind of work do you do?"

"I used to be an investment banker. Right now I'm treading that fine line between being retired and unemployed. A little consulting pays my bills. So I'm available for adventure."

"Won't be very adventurous sailing up the Intracoastal," I said. "But I can use somebody who's emotionally stable, comfortable around boats and ready to take off tomorrow."

"According to my ex, I'm not a paragon of stability, but I can manage the last two."

"I want you and I need you, so two out of three ain't bad. The job's yours."

"Anyone who can quote a Meat Loaf song is all right in my book," he said. "I'll take it."

We went over the details and I had him sign a bunch of forms, and then we stood up and shook hands. "I'll see you tomorrow morning at the dock," I said.

Our departure day dawned clear and sunny. Eddie arrived at the boatyard on the New River in downtown Fort Lauderdale by cab. "If I'd known you needed a ride, I'd have offered," I said, taking one of his big L.L.Bean duffels.

"I wasn't sure what the parking would be like here. It's no big deal."

He followed me down the dock, tugging his second duffel. "I brought too much with me," he said. "But I like having my own boat crap."

"Good idea. Especially with these transportation jobs, you never know whether there will be the kind of wrench you need. I travel pretty heavy myself."

He whistled as we approached the *Second Star*. "This is it?" he asked.

It was an impressive boat, and that's saying something, considering everything I've driven. "712 horsepower Cat C12 engines," I said. "40 horsepower bow and stern thrusters, three cabins with ensuite heads, and a four-sided flybridge enclosure with Lexan windows."

"I've been wasting my life with sailboats," he said as we stepped over the railing onto the teak transom.

"Stick with me, and you'll be spending a lot of time on boats like this." I led him below and we stowed his bags. After a tour of the boat we cast off and started east, moving slowly out past the finger islands of Las Olas Isles until we could turn into the waterway proper and start heading north.

"People sure know how to live down here," Eddie said as we passed one million-dollar home after another. We kept the speed down to between six and eight knots because of all the no-wake zones, passing the occasional sailboat or Jet Ski. The owner had specifically said we weren't to take the boat out into the open ocean, so we were restricted to the Intracoastal, also called "the Ditch."

We kept going north, past the mansions and high-rises of Palm Beach. I was navigating from inside the Portuguese bridge when Eddie went out onto the foredeck to check the ropes coiled there. He was sweating pretty fast in the warm spring air, and he pulled off his T-shirt, giving me an up close and personal look at his upper body.

It wasn't a bad view. He was stocky, with a stomach that was more round than flat, but his arms were well-muscled. His skin was smooth, with a trail of hair from between his pecs that led down to his waistline, and I could just see a tantalizing line of white where his tan died. My dick popped up but I tried to ignore it. I was over lusting after straight guys.

The rest of the day was a straightforward trip up the Ditch to Jensen Beach, where we stopped for the night at the Nettles Island Marina. I had stocked the fridge, so we fixed ourselves dinner and sat out on the deck to eat and drink.

It was a gorgeous sunset, the kind just made for sharing with someone you love. Unfortunately I was with Eddie Kanter, and though I could see myself falling in lust with his smooth back, his tight ass and what I guessed was a sizable dick, it wasn't going to happen. Just looking over at him made my own dick swell, and I had to shift my legs to cover it up.

"You make a mean mojito," Eddie said.

"The secret is the fresh mint," I said. "I grow it in my backyard, and I always pack some up whenever I travel."

"You ever bring women along as crew?" he asked.

"Sure. I know a bunch of women who can manage any kind of a boat."

"Seems like it would be hard to stay professional in a setting like this."

"Not a problem for me." I looked over at him. I hated hiding, and if I'd spent more than a half hour with Eddie before we embarked on this trip I'd have come out to him long before we got on the water. "I'm gay, Eddie. I hope that isn't a problem for you."

"You're gay?" He started to laugh.

The confusion must have shown on my face, because he stopped laughing. "Sorry. I've been trying so hard not to out myself all day because I thought you were straight and I was worried it would make you uncomfortable."

"But you were married," I said.

"I knew right away it was wrong, but I couldn't find my way out." He took a long drink of his mojito. "I did a lot of stupid things. Sex in men's rooms, at truck stops. When I traveled for business I'd find a gay bar, spend some money and get laid."

"Your wife never knew?"

"Not for a long time. Then a couple of years ago she started seeing a therapist to work out her issues. One of them was me, and the fact that I didn't show her any physical attention. She dragged me to see the therapist after a year, and it took less than a month of sessions before I told them both I was gay and wanted out of the marriage."

"That must have been tough."

"By that point it was a relief more than anything else. Fortunately I was making a lot of money, and it was easy to buy her off. I got myself an apartment in Manhattan and tried to start over again."

Heat lightning crackled across the landscape. At first I thought we were due for another storm, but after a few flashes I saw the difference. Heat lightning lights up the whole sky for a long second, darts around quickly like a little kid waving a sparkler. No long, thin wand of light and no thunder.

The sky flashed, electrifying the air around us. Or maybe that was sexual tension. I'll bet Eddie felt it, too, because he swallowed the last of his drink and stood up. "I'm going to hit the hay. See you in the morning."

I stayed up on deck for a while longer, nursing my drink, thinking about Eddie. My dick stiffened and pressed against my shorts as I thought about him stripping down in his cabin, sliding that smooth, naked body beneath the sheets. I was tempted to whip my dick out right then and take care of myself, but I resisted.

The next morning, the sky was streaked with red and heavy cumulus clouds hung over the barrier island that separated the Intracoastal from the Atlantic. "I figure we'll get as far as we can today," I said when Eddie and I began readying the boat to leave. "I'm not taking any chances, but I want to keep as close to the schedule as I can."

"Where are we headed?" he asked, as he untied the bow line.

"I have a reservation at a marina near Cape Canaveral," I said. "But if the storm gets heavy we'll just find a protected harbor and wait it out."

Eddie and I talked and joked as we worked, alternating steering and navigating. He was a comfortable partner to have around. I kept an eye on the storm clouds, always checking the charts for a place we could stop if we had to.

The storm came on us fast, when we were about halfway between safe harbors. We had no choice but to keep going, even though the rain was coming down in sheets and we had almost no visibility. Fortunately everyone else had enough sense to have already pulled into harbor. Eddie stayed out at the bow, making sure we stayed between the channel markers, and quickly he was soaked through.

The Intracoastal had widened out just south of Sebastian, and I didn't like being in the middle of so much open water when the rain was so heavy. I was relieved when I saw a harbor ahead of us and I was able to steer into shelter.

Eddie threw out the anchor and then came inside, dripping water. "I'd better get out of these clothes before I get the whole damn boat soaked," he said, pulling his polo shirt off over his head. I took it from him and began to wring it out in the kitchen sink. By the time I turned around again, he was naked, holding his shorts and boxers in one hand, his deck shoes in the other.

"I can take care of these," he said.

I looked him up and down. I'd already admired the smooth chest with the treasure trail of hair between his pecs, but now I could see that it led to a bush of wiry hair surrounding a generously sized penis, hanging half-hard. As I watched, it began to stiffen.

"How about that," I said, nodding downward. "Can I take care of that for you?"

He tossed the clothes and shoes into the sink and smiled, and I took that as an invitation. I got down on my knees on the stateroom carpet and slid my mouth over his dick. He tasted like salt water, sweat and male musk, and I loved it.

He groaned with pleasure. I started suctioning up and down on his dick, reaching up with one hand to fondle his nuts, then stroke his perineum. Quickly, though, he backed away. "I don't want to come so fast," he said. "The storm's still got a while to play out. How about if we go below and you get naked, too?"

"I like the way you think," I said, standing up. "My knees weren't going to last in that position for long anyway."

I led him down to the owner's cabin where I'd been sleeping, pulling off my shirt and kicking off my deck shoes as we went. When we got to the cabin he tugged me toward him and kissed me.

His chest was cold and wet and I wrapped my arms around him to warm him up. He got busy undoing my shorts and pushing them and my boxer briefs down to the deck, and we were both standing there naked, our stiff dicks pressed together as we hugged.

I backed away from him and took his hand. I lay down on the bed, him next to me, and we kissed again. It was nice to be with a guy who wanted to take things slow, and I explored his body with my fingers, looping one leg over his. He stroked and then pinched my nipples, and I arched my back with pleasure.

Then he went down on me, first slurping his tongue up and down my dick, then taking me in his mouth. I pushed his shoulder to turn him around, and we lay mouth to dick, both of us sucking for all we were worth. The boat was rocking in the waves, sliding us together and apart, making it a wild ride.

He came first; but then, I'd already warmed him up in the salon. I swallowed his load and then focused on my own pleasure. He kept on sucking me until I felt those shudders rising, and I squeezed my eyes closed and whimpered as I shot off in his mouth.

We cuddled until the wind died down. Then I stretched and said, "We'd better get back to work. I'd like to try for Canaveral if we can still make it."

He went back to his cabin to clean up and find dry clothes, and I found my clothes scattered around and dressed. He lifted the anchor and we went back out into the Ditch.

We worked quietly through the afternoon, neither of us saying anything more than necessary. I couldn't stop thinking about him, though. Rob, the bartender who was supposed to have joined me, gave great head and had a sexy, athletic body. But I always had the feeling he was going through the motions when we had sex.

Eddie, though, was a different story. I felt something from him I hadn't felt in a long time, a longing and a passion. But was it for me, or just because he'd been starved for dick? I didn't like not knowing.

The skies cleared, and by the time we docked at a marina south of Titusville, the air was fresh and slightly cool. We sat up on the deck with more mojitos. "How'd you end up down here?" I asked Eddie.

"I got tired of being invisible in New York. So I researched places where older gay men live. Provincetown's too cold. Scottsdale's too far from the ocean. So Wilton Manors won by default. I thought I'd move down here and there would be older guys lined up just looking for romance. My mistake. Turns out all the guys my age are partnered up, and the younger ones are just as shallow and self-obsessed as the ones in New York."

"Not all the guys your age," I said.

"What's your deal, then?" he asked. "You're a good-looking, stable guy. Why hasn't somebody snapped you up?"

I shook my head. "I had a bunch of short-term things, but none of them worked out for the long term."

"Why not?"

I wasn't going to put the blame on the losers I'd dated because the fault was probably mine as much as theirs. "I like my independence," I said. "And I'm not changing careers just so I can be somebody's regular date."

We both finished our drinks about the same time. "You want another?" I asked.

He shook his head. "I've got enough of a buzz. We should both probably get some sleep, anyway."

Was that going to be it? Or was he waiting for an invitation from me?

"I don't know how comfortable that crew bunk is," I said. "The bed in the owner's cabin is pretty choice, though."

"And it seemed big enough for the both of us earlier," Eddie said.

I stood up, and he followed me below. We were both kind of shy about stripping, though, now that the heat of passion was gone, and while he was in the head I got naked and slipped beneath the covers. I turned sideways to give him some privacy, and then he slid in beside me, naked, too. He put one arm over my shoulder and cuddled close, and we both fell asleep.

We woke at first light, both of us shy, and we dressed quickly and got under way. I wondered if Eddie was going to be the kind of guy who had to analyze everything about a relationship, or if he'd look at what we were doing just as sex.

But we quickly hit a lot of fishing traffic, and both of us had too much to do for idle chitchat. "They all come in bunches," Eddie said, standing beside me at the helm as a line of big sport fishermen rushed past us on their way out to the cut north of Anastasia State Park, to fight for amberjack and dolphin at the drop-off. "Like children playing follow the leader."

The *Second Star* rolled and pitched in their wake, and Eddie and I looked like cartoon drunks as we moved around the cabin and the decks. North of St. Augustine the water was dead calm, and for miles sometimes we were the only thing moving. Eddie made us sandwiches in the galley and brought them up to the Portuguese bridge.

"I don't want you to get the wrong idea," he said, between bites. "I'm not some kind of slut. I just...being trapped made me do stupid things. I'm trying not to do that kind of thing anymore."

"Yesterday," I said. "Was that a stupid thing?"

He shook his head. "Not for me. That was the smartest thing I've done in a long time."

I leaned over and kissed him lightly on the lips. "Me, too."

That night I blew up an air mattress and put it up on the bow. We were anchored just offshore and there were no other boats around. Eddie and I took our mojitos up there, stripped down, and after we finished toasting the gorgeous sunset, we made love out there in the open air. It was something I'd always wanted to do but never had the right combination of guy, gear and opportunity.

We were like a couple of kids, rolling around on each other, tickling and biting and laughing. I got to see what it felt like to have Eddie's chubby dick up my ass as I posed doggie-style on the mattress and he fucked me with long, sure strokes. The heat lightning lit up the sky in coruscating flashes, and it seemed like every time those bolts arced through the sky, Eddie hit yet another tender spot and sent similar reverberations through my body.

For the next couple of days, everything around us was flat. The low-lying marshes of northern Florida stretched out from the waterway in all directions, acres of green reeds that swayed gently as the water around them rippled and eddied in the wakes of passing boats. The sky was a silver gray the color of burnished aluminum.

We crossed into Georgia just after lunch, though only the charts told us so. I wondered what would happen to Eddie and me when the trip was over. Would I say good-bye to him at the airport, as I'd done so many times with other crew members? Or was there something between us that would last? I did my best to put those thoughts away and just enjoy the time we spent together.

On our last day, we left St. Simon's Island about an hour after sunrise, en route to Hilton Head. We were going to spend one last night on the boat and catch a flight from Savannah back to Fort Lauderdale the next morning.

We rounded a point, and suddenly there were dozens of seagulls trailing in our wake. Black-faced laughing gulls with white bodies and gray wings, and common gulls with white bodies and wings that were white close in and shaded out to a deep gray by their tips. They had little black beaks like the noses on miniature dogs.

We came into a sound, and the spray turned saltier. Most of the gulls followed a fishing boat out to sea, and Eddie went below. A pair of dolphins surfaced off the port bow, but disappeared before I could call him.

We passed a group of old shacks with ratty docks, all clustered together on a couple of hummocks of dry land. I was staring at a cemetery on Jekyll Island, noting the random pattern of azaleas in full bloom among the headstones, when I felt raindrops.

As the water intensified, Eddie came up to the Portuguese bridge to join me, and we passed a row of white mansions with round columns and formal porches facing the waterway. Live oaks hung with Spanish moss led down to little gazebos and docks at the water's edge. The rain was light and erratic for a while, and for nearly half an hour we saw distant lightning crackling twice as large as life. Low rumbles of thunder crashed across the marshes.

I checked the chart. We were about a mile south of a bascule bridge, and I radioed ahead a request for it to open, slowing the engines to a crawl so we wouldn't waste too much time waiting for it.

"Phil," Eddie said as I hung the radio mike up on its hook.

"Yeah?"

He shook his head. "Nothing."

We caught up to a tall sailboat that had already radioed for the bridge to open, and we scooted in behind it. On either side I saw the traffic backed up, people coming and going from the beach. I'd be one of those car-bound people again soon.

As we headed north, I looked back and saw both sides of the bridge lowering behind us. I tried not to see that as some kind of omen.

As we got closer to Hilton Head, young guys in fast cruisers with big engines darted back and forth in front of us in their hurry to return to port. They were followed by middle-aged good old boys and their wives and friends in pontoon boats, some with canopies and some without, all with coolers and six-packs and pink skin rosy from the sun and drink. Families in Bayliners out for a Sunday spin waved at teenaged boys in johnboats.

The rain began to fall in big splattery drops that beat down in a rhythmic pattern on the deck around us. We were only an hour out of Hilton Head and it seemed silly to stop. We were going slowly, and the visibility was still strong. By the time we were thoroughly drenched, flecks of sunlight began to hit the water and the rain let up. It was warm, and being wet felt good.

We entered the broad channel that led to Hilton Head and the sun came out. We checked in at the marina where they expected us, and we went through all the rigmarole of tying up ropes, laying out fenders and getting the boat situated. "What do we do now?" Eddie asked, when the final Styrofoam tube was in place.

"Clean up," I said. "Part of the deal is to leave the boat spick-and-span for the owners. Have to erase all the traces we were here."

"No pecker trails on the sheets," Eddie said.

"We'll wash those tomorrow morning," I said. "There's a laundry up at the marina office. And the owner left me a list of supplies to stock."

"Let's get started, then," Eddie said.

We worked in companionable silence for a couple of hours, and then Eddie went below to take a nap and I mixed myself a mojito with the last of the fresh mint and went up to the flying bridge. I finished my drink and thought about going below for another, when Eddie climbed up to join me.

"What are you doing?" he asked.

"Watching the heat lightning." I pointed to the sky, which lit up with a few obliging flashes. "There are storms far away from us—so far that we can't hear the thunder. But on summer nights something in the heat or the humidity diffuses the lightning and reforms it."

He nodded. "We've both been through a few storms." A brilliant flash off to his left illuminated his strong features for a second, glinting off the pendant around his neck.

"I can't change who I am at this point in my life," I said. "I love boats, and being out on the water. A handsome guy in my bed. A little adventure now and then."

"Sounds like a good combination."

"I have another transport on the books," I said. "Leaving in two weeks, Miami to Key West. Not as nice a boat as this one, but it'll be some fun. You think you'd like to join me?"

I didn't realize I was holding my breath until Eddie said, "You bet," and I let it out. Then we went below, to enjoy the spacious bed in the owner's cabin one last time.

RED ALERT: WEAPONS OF MASS ERECTION

Logan Zachary

The Russians are coming, the Russians are coming."

"Whoa, Paul Revere, what are you talking about?" I said into my cell phone after Billy Harris's excitement almost blew out my eardrum.

"The ship from Russia is here in the Duluth harbor, and the Russian sailors will be staying the night at Canal Park."

"And this affects me how?" I stood up and looked out my picture window with the view of Lake Superior and the lift bridge.

"They'll eat at Grandma's, probably head up to the Duluth Family Sauna, and then head back to their rooms to drink vodka and..."

"How do we fit in?" I saw the huge freighter floating just offshore.

"And we'll drink with them in their hotel room and then let them empty their sailor balls into us. Being at sea for such a long time, they'll want a hot ass to tap."

"Won't they want women?" I ran my hand through my blond curls and closed my eyes. What did he want with me now?

"Not all of them like women, and those are the hot, hairy, uncut ones we want."

"Aren't you working tonight?"

"Room service will never be the same when I'm done with my shift."

"So how do I fit into your scheme?" Why was I afraid I knew what he wanted me to do? I glanced at the clock: five-thirty Friday night.

"I want you to go scope out the boys at the Duluth Family Sauna. See which Russian longshoremen bat for our team."

I looked at my hazel eyes, tan skin, Finlander face. Why would a black-haired, bearded, hairy-chested Russian want me? Then again, why wouldn't he? "So I'm bait?"

"Master Bait, the best bait we have."

"In other words, you want me to use my gaydar to find us dates tonight."

"Bingo."

"You know I hate..."

"Please, please, please with sugar on it? With whipped cream on it?"

I walked up to the brick building at 18 North First Ave East. It was at the corner and looked down a steep sidewalk to downtown Duluth. A partial view of Lake Superior was visible between the buildings.

I entered the lobby and walked to the check-in desk.

Two older gentlemen sat behind the counter. One picked up a towel, washcloth and a bar of soap and set it on the counter as the other one stepped behind the old-fashioned cash register and said, "Hello. What would you like today?"

I looked at the sign.

Duluth Family Sauna Rates:
Private Room: $13.00 single, $18.95 couple, $9.00 seniors
Day Pass: $16.00, no re-admittance.
All Day Pass: $20.00 come and go as you please.
Saturday Sleepover: $32.00 Sat noon to Sunday 8 am.
Late Night Saturday: $22.00 Sat 9 pm to Sunday 8 am.

I opened my wallet and pulled out a twenty. "I'll just take a day pass."

The man behind the cash register pushed a few buttons, the register dinged and the wooden drawer opened up. He pulled out four singles and handed them to me as he took my twenty. "Head down those stairs, find an empty locker and have fun."

"Play safe," the other man said as he handed me the stack. A gold-foil-wrapped condom sat on top of the bar of soap. He must have added that when I wasn't looking. "There are more downstairs if you need them." His eyes looked me up one side and down the other. "I'm sure you'll need a lot more." He reached under the counter and added another condom to my pile.

"Thanks." I balanced my possessions and went down the dark stairwell to the bull pen. The staircase turned and another flight opened into the locker room. The slam of a metal locker welcomed me as I stepped onto the black rubber mat. A bank of lockers lined two walls, and I headed to one that stood open. I set the towel on the wooden bench, kicked off my shoes, and set them on the rusted floor of the locker. I removed my socks and set them on top. I pulled my red polo shirt over my head and started to undo my fly as I noticed a handsome man watching me.

He licked his full lips and smiled.

I smiled back and removed my jeans and hung them on a hook. Standing in my white briefs, I turned my back to him and slipped them off. I dropped them on my shoes and reached for my towel. Trying to keep my dick covered, I swung my towel around my narrow waist. I tied a knot with the loose ends and noticed a huge bulge in front.

The man nodded at me. "You're a big boy, aren't you? I have a private room upstairs if you want to see it." He pulled his towel back to reveal a huge penis and large dangling balls.

I smiled and almost wiped my mouth with the back of my hand. "I'm meeting a friend," I said, "but your offer is most appetizing. I would enjoy a rain check."

The man waved me over and said, "Aren't we all?" He ran his hand under my towel and massaged me. He ran his hand along my shaft and rolled my balls between his fingers. He withdrew it and brought it to his nose and inhaled deeply. "Ah," he said, and sucked on his finger. He then slipped it back under the towel and maneuvered between my cheeks.

I nodded.

He applied a little pressure and entered me. His thumb bounced my balls as he pushed in and pulled out of my ass.

My knees went weak and threatened to collapse, but the sensation warmed me from the inside out. I pressed down on his hand. My cock swelled and oozed precum. A wet spot formed on the sheer white towel.

He withdrew his finger and inserted two.

I widened my stance and rode his hand. My cock lifted the towel and slipped out under the edge. The fat mushroom end glistened as a pearl of precum formed in the opening. As it grew, the cream slowly rolled down my thick shaft.

His huge dick rubbed along my hairy leg.

I felt a thick, warm liquid run down to my foot.

"The Russians are coming, the Russians are coming" filtered through my mind as my balls were saying, "We're coming, we're coming." A huge load shot out of my cock and landed on his oozing dick.

He reached up and milked my cock as his fingers dug into my ass and tapped my prostate, pushing out more cum. He scooped up my seed and smeared it along his dick, jacking it hard. He shot his wad along my leg, thick cream glazing my leg hair.

"Sorry to set you off so fast." He looked down at his dick. "Mine takes a while to reload."

I looked down at my leg. "I'll get to hit the showers first off." I tucked my cock back into my towel. "Thanks, I needed that, and you sure got my night off to a good start." I walked over to the tiled shower room and turned on the water. The head burst to life with cold water, and I jumped out of the way until it warmed up. Steam slowly filled the room and I stuck my foot into the spray, washing the cum down the floor drain.

I pulled the towel off and rinsed off my cock. The warm water felt great, bringing me to semi-wood. I turned off the water and wrapped the towel around my waist.

There was a maze of yellow-green walls that formed cubicles with doors and glory and peep holes, an empty bed in that one, a man lying face-down to my right. I looked in a peek hole to see a man motion for me to join him. I smiled and pointed to the steam room.

The fog coated the glass door, and the heavy scent of eucalyptus hung in the air, covering the bleach scent. I opened the door and a wall of steam floated out. A shadow moved as I entered the room. A layer of mist coated my body, and the towel hung damp around my waist, clinging to me like a second skin.

The man was naked and upside down on the bench. His head hung down over the bottom seat as his legs were spread wide, and he was working his dick.

"Excuse me," I said and backed out of the room.

He opened his mouth wide and licked his lips. "Come back."

"Sorry, looking for a friend." I let go of the door as it swung shut.

"I can be your friend..." And the door closed.

I went over to the sauna and pulled the door open, and a heat wave blasted me as I entered. The heavy scent of wood smoke hung in the air. A dim lightbulb illuminated the room; three levels of wooden benches lined three of the walls. No one was inside. I stepped up to the second level with my bare feet and felt the heat soak into my soles. I picked up the wooden ladle and threw water on the barrel of Lake Superior rocks. Steam hissed as the water sizzled on the hot stones and evaporated immediately.

A new wave of humid heat hit me, and I felt like my hair was on fire. I patted it and found it safe, glad I wasn't on the top bench. I found a corner spot and sprinkled some water on the seat and sat down. My damp towel absorbed the water, cooling the bench only slightly. Pouring more water over my feet made the wood safe to rest them on.

Sweat ran out of every pore on my body. I breathed in deeply, savoring the humidity and wood smoke. Only a real Finnish sauna smelled like this. I closed my eyes and absorbed the calm.

The sauna door's hinge squealed as it opened.

I opened my eyes and watched as a man entered. He was a

good looking middle-aged guy, a few extra pounds, otherwise in great shape. He saw me staring at him and he said, "You know the Russians are coming."

I smiled to myself. Was I the only one in town who didn't follow the Russian invasion? "That's what I heard."

"You'd better get out of here before they enter."

"Why?"

"You're a good-looking blond. They'll gang-rape you in here."

Images of that made my cock start to swell again. Two big hairy guys, using my body, fucking every opening I had, stuffing in their thick uncut cocks, thick, black hair on their chests and asses.

Let Billy find his own date tonight, I thought, but said, "I'm sure I can hold my own."

The man rolled his eyes, not believing me. "Suit yourself, but don't say I didn't warn you. I just wanted to get my sauna done and get out of here before they arrive." He poured a ladleful of water on the rocks and steam rose, as did the heat.

I inhaled the hot humidity and felt another wave of sweat break out over my body. I tentatively sat back and tested the wall. Too hot to touch with my bare skin.

Fifteen minutes passed, the man left, and my body felt like a wet noodle, limp and relaxed. I needed to cool off and close all my pores. I headed to the shower and stepped into the cold spray, rinsing all the salty sweat and fatigue away.

Just as I finished the shower three big, hairy men came into the shower room.

"You must shower first," the beefy man said as he pulled his towel off his narrow hips. His back was as furry as his chest, thick black curls covered his body and a huge uncut penis swung between his legs.

The other two men spoke rapidly in Russian. They snapped each other with their towels and made obscene gestures to each other and the other Russian. They washed quickly and wrapped their towels around their waists.

"We'll do the sauna and then the steam bath. After that we head back to the hotel for the night."

"Do we bring someone back?" one asked in broken English.

The older man answered in Russian, and I didn't understand the word.

The three departed the showers and I headed to my locker. I knew what they looked like, so I was ready to leave.

A blond man streaked into the locker area and ripped open his locker. "The Russians are coming." He dressed and fled.

I dried off and left soon behind him. I drove down to Canal Park and parked.

Billy waited at the front desk and smiled as he saw me. "Did you make contact?"

"I saw them in all their glory, but a lot of guys took off as they arrived."

Billy ran his hand through his hair and pulled it back. "I've heard stories about what they did in the sauna…"

I stood watch at the hotel's front door and nodded to Billy when the three arrived.

He watched as the men walked by. As they entered the elevator, I rushed over to the front desk. "I know exactly which rooms they are in." He looked at the clock. "I'm off in twenty minutes, so when they call for room service, we'll be ready." He undid his pants and quickly pulled them off.

"What are you doing?"

"I'm changing before my shift is over, so I'll be ready."

He pulled out a pair of tight, faded jeans and paused for a moment.

"What's wrong?"

"With or without underwear?" he asked me.

Someone was coming up the walkway to the front door. I saw them reach for the handle. "With," I said.

Billy stepped into the jeans as the door opened. He zipped and buttoned before the guest walked by.

I let out the breath I had been holding.

"Relax, they can't see behind the desk. I could be buck-ass naked behind here from the waist down and no one would be any the wiser."

Charlie came to the front desk and started to prepare for the night. "How's it going?" He saw Billy hurrying to get ready. "Are the Russians here again?"

Billy nodded.

"Damn, they're so demanding." Charlie put his backpack under the front desk and started to get ready for his shift.

Billy picked up two huge bottles of vodka.

"Thank you Jesus," Charlie said. "My shift will be a breeze."

Billy unbuttoned his shirt and switched it.

The front desk phone rang and Charlie answered it.

"Send vodka up to room 315," a loud foreign man's voice demanded.

"Right away, sir," Charlie said, and hung up. "You're on, vodka for 315."

Billy handed me a bottle and he took one. He padded his back pocket. "Don't wait up for us." And we headed for the elevators.

"Just follow my lead, and we'll party all night." Billy unbuttoned his top two buttons as we rode up.

Room 315 stood across from the elevator. We got off and knocked on the door. It opened and the older Russian man ushered us in.

Billy walked in without a pause, I took a few halting steps and then followed.

The man closed the door and said, "Pour and drink with us."

Billy was already setting up five glasses and cracking the seal on his bottle. He poured generous servings into them and motioned for me to hand them out.

I picked up two and took them to the men in the one bed. One looked passed out but the other one reached eagerly for the glass.

Billy took two and handed one to the older man. He looked at the last glass and I hurried over to it. As I picked it up, Billy raised his glass and said, "To the sailors of the Great Lakes."

Everyone lifted his glass and said, *"Skål."*

"To the Great Lake," Billy said, "Lake Superior."

Everyone drank.

"To Russia," I said.

Everyone drank.

"To Moscow, to United States, to men, to women…" To whoever they said, we drank.

I know I took small sips, if any, but the Russians drank and needed their glasses refilled after two toasts.

I opened my bottle as Billy's ran dry.

The one who looked unconscious when we came in was out cold. His bed mate took off his shirt and showed us his tattooed back and arms. His chest was hairy like the older one, but his back was smooth, covered in art: the Kremlin in all its glory. He unbuckled his pants and sat on the edge of the bed. He slapped the bed and waved me over.

Billy took his shirt off and unbuckled his jeans. He poured

vodka down his chest, and the older Russian licked it off. He licked up to his nipple and sucked on that. Billy lay back on his bed and filled his belly button with vodka.

The older Russian took off his shirt, showing his hairy torso, and positioned his mouth over Billy's navel. He licked inside once and then sealed his lips around it and drank.

"Na zdorovye," he said.

Billy filled his navel again.

This time the man missed his belly and caught the mushroom head of his cock through the cotton of Billy's underwear. He sucked on it through the material. When he came up, Billy's underwear was almost see-through and his cock had tripled in size.

The Russian drank from his belly button and pointed again.

Billy kicked off his jeans and refilled. Vodka ran down his belly to his underwear's waistband. He adjusted his briefs and a hairy ball fell out of the leg opening.

The Russian saw this and dove for it. He drew it into his mouth and rolled it with his tongue.

Billy tried to sit up, but the older man pushed him down before he could spill any of the clear fluid. The Russian pulled off Billy's briefs and tossed them to the floor, bent forward and drank his body shot and took the bottle from Billy's hand. He poured vodka on his dick and quickly licked it off. He brought the bottle to his lips and drank, filling his mouth, then took Billy's willy into his mouth and sucked on it.

Billy squirmed on the bed, but the big hairy Russian held him in place.

My Russian had seen enough, and now it was his turn to play. He took the bottle from my hand and pushed me down on the bed. He pulled my pants off and said, "Be a sailor, see the world," and then he filled my navel with vodka.

The cold liquid splashed on my belly and filled my belly button. Excess alcohol ran over me in all directions.

"*Skål,*" he said and dove for my belly.

He drank and then rolled me over onto my stomach. He rubbed along my spine, and I tensed. I felt a cool liquid run down my spine and pool in the hollow above my butt. He stopped pouring and drank. I felt his fingers pull my underwear down and expose my ass. My buttcheeks tensed together as he poured vodka down my cleft. The alcohol ran down my crack and settled in the hollow.

My Russian licked down my crease and slurped the vodka. He spread my cheeks and licked down to my hole. His rough tongue tasted my sensitive pucker and he twirled around and around, trying to get deeper.

I arched my back and opened myself to him.

He poured my vodka and drank.

I looked over to the other bed with Billy.

He sat on the hairy Russian's lap and rode him like a horse. "The Russians are coming, the Russians are coming." Billy's eyes rolled back in his head as he bounced harder and harder on his cock.

I felt the lip of the vodka bottle touch my hole as he tried to pour alcohol into my ass.

"Relax, you like, I like." His thick accent resonated.

If he wanted to drink out of my ass, whatever; I arched my back more and spread my cheeks. I tried to relax as he slipped the neck into me. I was glad it was the smaller of the two bottles. Cold liquids filled me up, and the pressure grew deep inside.

He pulled the bottle out and inserted a straw. He sucked hard, and I felt the pressure slowly release. He drank his fill and pulled the straw out and kissed my pucker. "Ahh." He wiped his mouth with the back of his hand. He slapped my ass and said, "And now we fuck."

He unzipped his pants the rest of the way and pulled them off. He wore baggy boxers, and a huge bulge tented the front. His hairy chest filtered down into a thicker bush above his waistband. He pulled them off, and his eight-inch cock sprang out. It slapped his belly and bounced up and down. "You like?" The foreskin dripped with precum as he stuck his cock in front of my face.

Before he could choke me with it, I grabbed his thick girth and stroked it a few times. I licked his rutter and pulled his foreskin back. His mushroom head appeared and disappeared as I stroked his cock.

He pushed his hips forward and bent over my body. He pulled my briefs off the rest of the way, and as soon as he saw my cock, he dropped to his knees and worked on my nine. He licked my balls and in the crease between my ball and leg.

Our sleeping bedmate rolled over and his hand landed on my chest. He played with my nipple for a few seconds and fell back asleep.

I felt a finger explore my ass as my Russian sucked on me. I relaxed and allowed him to penetrate me.

His finger slipped in and out as some vodka trickled out too.

My head began to tingle and spin as he deep-throated my cock.

His thumb rolled my balls as he drew down hard on me.

I could feel the buzz growing, and then realized it was the alcohol he had poured into my ass hitting into my blood stream, and not what I drank. Damn, so much for staying in control. I looked over at Billy. He was passed out and lay sprawled on the other bed. The naked Russian saw my gaze and rose. His huge uncut cock stood straight out in front of him like a proud masthead, and he sailed toward my harbor.

My Russian stopped sucking on my dick and argued with the older man for a few seconds and moved his bare ass over and allowed him to join in. My man looked at his bed mate and pushed him with both hands.

His partner rolled over the edge of the bed and hit the floor without waking up. My Russian climbed over me and took his place.

Billy's Russian kissed me, gently at first and then deep and probing. His tongue entered my mouth as he worked his finger into the other end.

My cock was inside a hot mouth, and every nerve fiber seemed to be involved. I curled my toes as they played with me. I tasted vodka and smelled hot male desire. The alcohol washed away any inhibition I had.

I rolled onto my left side, and Billy's sailor spooned my ass. He kept kissing my ear and stuck his tongue inside. His torpedo slipped between my cheeks and sought out its hot target.

The mouth slowly sucked along my cock and retracted to the tip. His tongue explored the slit and circled the head. He opened the bedside table and pulled out two condoms, passed one over me to the other sailor and kept one for himself. He ripped the cellophane open with his teeth and rolled the rubber, placed it over my cock's end and rolled it down my shaft.

Behind me, the older man donned his condom and grasped my hips. Sailor sandwich? Cream filling to a Russian Oreo? And he was inside me. The pain disappeared as fast as it came.

My sailor guided his butt to my cock. He pushed back, and I was inside him.

A wave started behind me and flowed through me and into him. Pelvis to pelvis to pelvis, ebb and flow, insertion, retraction, just float.

I reached forward and grabbed his cock. My fingers combed through his bush and rolled his balls. Precum flowed out of him and lubed my hand for smooth sailing. I humped his rump as my butt was trolled.

My ear was sucked and the rate of our hips doubled. More precum flowed over my hand and I jacked faster.

He pushed his ass onto my cock, and I followed suit on the captain's cock, encouraging him, and he took it. Our rhythm sped up and the pleasure drove me faster, deeper. My cock felt ready to explode, and I wanted that to happen inside my ass. "Harder," I said.

No one resisted. Our waves grew bigger and bigger. The tension grew in me, and I rowed faster on the cock in my hand. I dove into him hard and felt him capsize, spilling his load all over my hand and across his bed.

My balls released in sync and I plunged in deeper and harder, sending all my swimmers into the rubber. I tensed on the one behind me and a second later, he was drooling in my ear and spasming in my ass. We clung to each other as the waves washed over us, finishing the collective orgasm that bobbed between us.

Slowly, we retracted our tentacles, and all was as it started. My sailor rolled over and fell asleep. Billy's captain headed back to his bed. I slowly stood and found my land legs. I dressed and looked over at Billy. Leave him or take him with?

I slipped his pants and shoes on, sat him up and pulled his shirt around his back. Who knew where his underwear was, and I wasn't going to look for it. The Russians could have it. I drag-carried him out of the room to the elevator.

As we stepped off, Charlie waved me over. "Bring him to the employee lounge." He led the way.

I deposited him on a couch and smiled at Charlie. "Thanks."

"I swear he sleeps here more than he does at his home."
Charlie clicked his tongue as we left.

The sex had burned off most of the vodka, and I was safe
to drive home. I parked in the driveway and shed my clothes as
I walked through the house. I drank a tall glass of water and
took two aspirins. Dropping to bed naked felt so good; the
sheets were cool and clean. I inhaled deeply and drifted off to
sleep.

My cell phone rang a few minutes later, and I rolled over
and answered it. "Hello?"

"The Russians are coming, the Russians are coming,
again."

And I hung up the phone.

CROATIAN SAIL

Jay Starre

G rant met Andrej in Dubrovnik. Climbing a stepped lane that served as a street in the upper part of that Croatian city, he first spotted him among the profusion of potted plants that hugged the centuries-old buildings on either side of the stairs.

He looked like he was a college student, with shoulder-length straight blond hair and a small blond goatee. His casual shorts, light shirt and sandals were a little on the expensive side, though, and on closer inspection he also looked a little older than Grant first guessed—maybe closer to his own age of twenty-seven.

Hazel eyes under blond brows looked directly at him as the stranger offered a crooked smile, one corner of his upper lip curling. He was cute and sexy.

And he was interested. *"Bonjour,"* he said brightly.

"Uh, hello. Do you speak English? I'm American and sadly not too good with languages," Grant immediately confessed.

"Ah, very good. I do speak English quite okay. I am Andrej and I am Croatian."

"Wow! A local. Maybe you could show me around. You're definitely hotter than the usual tour guides..." He offered his brightest smile and left it at that. If Andrej was put off by the come-on, it was too bad. At least he'd played his cards.

The Croatian laughed easily and reached out to place a hand on Grant's shoulder. That hand settled over the area where his tank top left bare flesh exposed. Flesh on flesh. Andrej squeezed lightly and looked directly into his golden eyes. "I will be glad to do so. How would you like to go for a sail? I have my boat in the harbor and my day is free. So is my night. Okay, Mr. Cute American?"

Dazzled by the gorgeous hazel eyes gazing into his own and the gentle hand warming his shoulder, Grant felt a hard-on rising in his shorts. He was ready to agree to just about anything. But sailing?

"Uh, awesome. But I've never sailed before."

"Do not worry. I am a good sailor. Come, I will show you my boat and you will decide."

Grant shouldn't have worried about being too bold. This dude was that in spades, and spontaneous too it seemed. Exactly what he was looking for. A high school biology teacher in Des Moines, he'd grown disillusioned with his staid lifestyle. He seemed to have everything under control in his life, yes, but that was the problem. Too much control, not enough chaos. "Wow. Sure. I'm all yours, Andrej."

That hand remained on his shoulder as the fair-haired Croatian turned him around and they descended the greenery-lined lane amidst the few other tourists who dared the morning climb—and locals who thought it ordinary.

"Here, Mr. Cute American. This is a pleasant view, yes?"

Andrej steered Grant off the lane onto a little side patio that jutted out above the roofs of the city below.

"Amazing! I'm Grant, by the way. Sorry I didn't say so earlier."

"It is okay. There, that house with the palm tree just to the right. That is my family's home."

Grant spotted the building amidst a sea of other red-tiled roofs. Some of those roofs were obviously much newer than the rest, and he understood why. The war of independence from Yugoslavia in the early '90s included a brutal shelling of this historic city, thus the newer roofs.

"My family has lived in this house for three hundred years."

This was a stunning notion for Grant. "Amazing. How old is the house?"

"Five hundred years. And the wall you see all around the city? It was mostly built in the fourteenth century. Dubrovnik was a major maritime power and a rival to Venice during the fifteenth century and managed to remain independent right up to the nineteenth century. The salt trade and shipbuilding were our city's mainstays. That wall, huge underground granaries and water piped in from the mountains, along with crafty diplomacy, saved us from being swallowed up by invaders for many, many centuries. Marvelous, yes?"

The setting was as dramatic as its history. Palm trees rose amidst the red tiles while the architecture was a pleasant mix of Renaissance and Gothic, and the wall, still intact, surrounded it all. The city jutted out into the harbor, where Adriatic waters sparkled in the morning sunlight. Behind them, a mountain rose defiantly. Grant could picture the town bustling with life and looking much the same hundreds of years earlier.

"We call our city the Pearl of the Adriatic. But come, we shall sail away together and I will show you more wonders of Croatia!"

Andrej laughed and squeezed Grant's shoulder again. The American's cock was definitely hard by this time, and he hoped it wasn't too obvious bulging in his shorts.

By the time they reached the harbor below, the morning stillness had evaporated and a brisk breeze had sprung up, which Andrej appreciated but which made Grant a little apprehensive.

"Wonderful! We shall have a good sail today."

Painted emerald green, the boat was smaller than Grant had imagined. It was not more than maybe twenty feet long, with two sails draped from the mast. He wondered when he should reveal to his hot new friend how little he knew about sailboats, or any boats.

"It is beautiful, no? I built it myself. Well, my family helped. We have been shipbuilders for a long time."

"Three hundred years?"

"Maybe more!"

They both laughed and Grant was pleased that Andrej had a sense of fun about himself.

That would help. As they prepared to step off the dock and into the deck of the slightly rocking boat below, he was definitely growing nervous.

"It's not that I'm afraid of sailing…it's just that I'm afraid of boats," Grant blurted out.

Andrej took his hand and helped him down, smiling up at him. "There is nothing to worry about. It will be a little rough out in the open water, but soon we will be protected between the islands and the mainland. You will see. If you have never sailed, then you are in for a brilliant experience."

The Croatian had a very soothing voice, not especially deep but very engaging with a gentle lilt. He was also drop-dead gorgeous. Dazzled, Grant found himself seated at the back end and being handed a life jacket before he knew it.

He watched with awe as Andrej did everything necessary to get them out of their berth and into the open water of the harbor. He untied them from the dock and expertly rowed them away from it with the large oars. That's when Grant realized there was no engine.

"What if the wind dies down? Do we have to row?"

"Yes. You look very strong, Mr. Cute American. I will let you do the rowing, yes?"

He laughed as he stowed the oars and slipped back to sit beside Grant on the bench in the rear of the boat. Then, with some cranking on a winch and releasing of ropes, the mainsail billowed in the wind, snapped taut and they leapt forward.

"Wow! It goes faster than I imagined!"

The wind whipped past them as they carved a magnificent curve across the harbor and out into the Adriatic. "We're going north! Hold on tight, Mr. American!"

His fear of boating was put to the test. The brisk wind at their backs not only filled the two sails with its energetic force, it whipped up the waves ahead of them. The little sailboat leaped and bounded over those waves, up and down, slamming against the water like a jackhammer, rising up again, then slamming down, over and over.

It was exhilarating. He gripped the seat fiercely, but was comforted by the look of absolute glee on Andrej's face, rather than rictus of terror he imagined he displayed. As well, the sailor's bare knee often pressed against his own and a free hand even dropped to squeeze it once.

"Brilliant, no?" Andrej shouted to him.

"Awesome! Scary as hell and awesome," he yelled back.

Even though the view of the shore was rising and falling along with the leaping of the boat, he did take note of its dramatic beauty. High mountains were covered with scrub evergreen oak or barren with stone. There were vineyards with stone terraces, olive orchards, almond orchards and sheep bleating as they ran up the rocky slopes. And it changed by the mile.

In the midst of that slamming violence, Andrej turned to Grant and leaned over to kiss him. It was unexpected and took him off guard, but he managed to release his knuckle-whitening grip with one hand and reach around the Croatian to seize the back of his neck and hold him tight against his mouth.

The kiss was as fierce as the exhilarating leap of the boat beneath them. Tongues exchanged places, lips sucked and slobbered. But it was brief as Andrej pulled away and got back to the business of preventing them from capsizing and drowning.

Grant watched Andrej as he cranked the winch and laughed as the mainsail collapsed. The boom swung across the deck, and the sail then billowed outward again and they veered east-ward. His bare arms were tanned and muscular, with just a down of blond. Just like his legs. Very sexy. The memory of that unexpected kiss lingered along with the promise of more. Now he couldn't care less if they ended up shipwrecked on some desolate shore, as long as Andrej was there with him!

Andrej laughed again, then leaned in for another quick kiss.

The rest of the morning passed in a sublime flow of exchanged kisses and light caresses, a sensual foreplay amidst the stun-ning scenery of the Croatian shoreline. They passed fish and oyster farms amongst inlets and islands. Small medieval towns appeared on little peninsulas or nestled in small bays, as if they had been transported to another time and place. Other boats of all kinds sailed or motored past them in either direction. Andrej sailed them steadily forward in the light breeze, taking full advantage of his sailing skills to propel them across the rippled surface.

Finally they slowed and sailed gently past a half-submerged wreck. Its rusted bottom was clearly visible in the sparkling aquamarine water. Andrej maneuvered them into a small cove behind that wreck where high cliffs rose dramatically on all sides.

Grant was not aggressive by nature and allowed Andrej to lead. He was totally content to kiss and grope, completely clothed with their life jackets between them. There seemed to be no rush, especially with the placid sea around them, the quiet of the cliffs and the serenity of the wreck blocking the view of the open water and any passing boats.

Andrej was an excellent kisser. He wasn't shy about diving in with his tongue, or sucking with loud slurps and smacks, but he was also into the softer strokes of tongue on lips and gentle nipping of teeth on darting tongue. And his hands were equally exciting. He ran them up and down Grant's bare arms, along his calves and knees, and slid them up along his thighs under his baggy shorts. He even settled a hand over Grant's crotch to squeeze and massage his stiff cock.

Grant felt Andrej's smooth skin as well, reveling in the soft down and the absolute firmness of the muscle. He was less bold about groping cock, until Andrej took his hand and placed it directly over it. He squeezed the lengthy pole and imagined what it looked like once free of his shorts and underwear.

"Shall we continue? The day is not quite over yet."

Catching the light breeze expertly, Andrej maneuvered them back into the channel between islands and they tacked north again, zigzagging their way to fresh scenery and new waters.

It was amazing to Grant how the islands and coast varied so much from mile to mile. Each island was a world unto itself, and the towns they passed hugging the shore were fascinating relics of a centuries-old culture while still thriving in a modern-day world.

It was also amazing to him how the wind propelled them along so effortlessly. Effortlessly on his part, as he mostly watched Andrej do the work. He had never thought of the wind in that particular way, an energy source that could be harnessed to suit one's pleasure. Mostly it was a nuisance—and downright dangerous when it brought tornadoes to Iowa.

"Here is where we will spend the night. Is this okay? We can instead find a harbor and sleep in a hotel, if that is your preference."

The blond Croatian directed them into a small bay along a vineyard-lined coast. Oaks overhung the rocky shore and created a little haven of calm privacy. He threw out an anchor, then with Grant's help tied a rope to a jutting boulder on the shore to their left. They secured the boom so it wouldn't move across the deck like it had been doing all day long.

"Will we sleep in the boat?" he dared to ask.

"Yes. You will find it very pleasant. And so will I, Mr. Cute American."

They made a bed of sorts with their life jackets and blankets that had been stowed in a watertight container near the prow. By the time they had done all this, the sun had set behind the island and they were treated to the glow of a rising moon across the water in the east.

"Tell me about yourself, Grant. I am Croatian for centuries, but you? Americans are many things, I believe."

They cuddled together on the low deck beside one of the oars, still dressed. Grant revealed himself with slightly deprecatory simplicity. "I was born in Iowa, grew up there, went to college there and now I teach high school there. Not completely unusual, but not exactly common in the mobile U.S. My father is mainly Irish, but with a great-grandfather who was a black American slave. My mother is a Mexican immigrant, and so she's part Spanish and part Native American. I am a mongrel, which is typical of Americans."

Andrej laughed. "That explains your lovely black hair and dark tan. And your lovely full lips and lovely broad nose and lovely big golden eyes…" and his words trailed off as he leaned in to kiss Grant in the moonlight.

It was a gentle kiss, with none of the rushed excitement of some of their earlier ones exchanged during the flight of their sail over the water. They stroked each other's bare arms and tongued each other's lips, all to the gentle rocking of the boat.

Andrej rose, pulling Grant to his knees with him. Grant found it amazing how already he'd grown accustomed to shifting his body weight to compensate for the movement of the boat, out of fear perhaps that he would cause it to capsize, but also as a natural thing almost like walking or running.

The Croatian smiled as he lifted the bottom of Grant's tank top and pulled it up over his head. The American lifted his arms, feeling a little tingle as his bare pits were exposed and Andrej teased him by dipping into his left one and stroking the sensitive area with his tongue.

"Yikes! That tickles." He giggled then groaned as Andrej began to suck and slurp the raised pit with lips and tongue.

Grant was smooth under there, and practically everywhere else. Not that he bothered to shave anywhere but his face; he was just naturally hairless. Now Andrej's lips easily slid out of that pit and over his muscular chest to find and settle on one nipple—and suck.

"Oh god. Oh yeah," he muttered as he dared to reach down and return Andrej's earlier favor by pulling up on the tail of his tank top and lifting it off.

Their bodies were very different. Grant ran his hands over the blond's slim back as Andrej continued to suck on his nipple, even nipping it lightly before he engulfed the other with wet lips. Grant was broad and almost muscle-bound. He had played football in high school and turned to weight training in college. He still worked out in the gym regularly.

His fingers slid all over the bare flesh of Andrej's back, shoulders and neck as he gasped and shuddered under that nipple assault. He had never had his nipples so expertly sucked! In fact, most of his sexual encounters had been plain suck-and-fuck, not very inventive, and never, ever so sensually satisfying.

In the moonlight, in the bottom of a boat on the Adriatic Sea with the coast of Croatia a few yards away, it couldn't have been more romantic. And this guy, he was not normal. Certainly he was beautiful to look at, but so were many others. It was something more than mere physical looks about him that affected Grant so powerfully.

But for now, it was the purely physical sensation of tongue and lips slowly sliding down his six-pack abs that had him groaning. Fingers found the buttons of his fly and opened them as tongue delved into his navel and he arched upward toward it. Another first!

He was slowly stripped as lips gently kissed him further down, and further down. He rolled backward and raised his feet and hips as his shorts, then underwear were pulled off. He was naked, and Andrej's tongue began lapping at the head of his stiff cock.

"Yes! Thank you, Andrej! That feels amazing...amazing!"

The Croatian said nothing, his mouth and hands doing all the talking. His tongue dipped into Grant's piss slit, rubbing it playfully while the dark-haired American groaned and pushed upward into it. The tongue swabbed all over his cock head before descending along the thick shaft to stroke all over it and around it. Grant humped Andrej's chin and nose and cheeks, growing more and more bold and less and less inhibited.

There definitely was something about the Croatian that brought out the adventurous side of him. He suddenly didn't feel the need to pretend, or explain himself, or try to impress. He grabbed hold of his own full asscheeks and spread them, offering up his smooth crack and hole.

Andrej chuckled appreciatively deep in his throat as his tongue darted downward and settled directly on the quivering sphincter. It licked, then stabbed, then stroked. Grant's thighs shook and his feet in the air wobbled. He couldn't stop moaning and groaning.

The Croatian licked back upward along the ridge of Grant's perineum, then over his dangling balls. He opened wide and sucked in one, then the other. With a mouthful of nuts, he took hold of Grant's cock with one hand and probed his spit-gobbed hole with the other.

"Oh my god...oh yeah...whatever you want, Andrej...do it!"

And he meant it. A fingertip wormed its way past a quivering butt rim and slowly buried itself. A fist on his cock stroked it up and down. The mouth surrounding his balls sucked and teased before abandoning them and returning to the base of his cock. Lips and tongue replaced that fist as he began an amazing suck job. Mouth engulfed cock head, then slowly dropped down to swallow shaft to the root. Wet and warm, that mouth vacuumed rhythmically before rising to concentrate on the fat head. Tongue twirled over it as lips massaged it.

The finger in his ass rotated and pulled. It worked in and out, delving for prostate and teasing it. The other hand found one of his nipples and began to tug at it, then lightly pinch it. Grant shuddered and whimpered, so many exquisite sensations rocking him he didn't know which to focus on.

He grabbed his own feet and pulled them back and out to the sides, wide open for Andrej's assault. The Croatian devoured him. He sucked cock, licked balls and crack and ate ass. His hands alternated between cock, nipples and asshole.

The moon was full and bathed them with pale light. Grant gazed down at the blond head buried between his thighs and felt his heart move. This, maybe, was how love started! He almost laughed at the notion as Andrej's tongue twirled deep between his puckered asslips, but then immediately abandoned that cynical train of thought.

As if reading his mind, the Croatian came up for air and rose up to stare down at him. "Can I fuck you, Mr. Cute American? I have the condoms and the lubricant."

"I have them too, in my pack," Grant admitted with a giggle.

"This means yes, no?"

"Yes!"

Grant lay back and watched, his feet back on the deck beneath them as Andrej finished undressing, his very long cock rearing up between his slim thighs and jerking with excitement as he rolled a condom down over it. He handed Grant a small bottle of lube and nodded.

He understood. Lifting his feet again, his ass was once more wide open. Andrej moved in close to kneel between his raised feet, the boat rocking then settling. Grant squirted slippery lube into his own crack, feeling it dribble down over his well-fingered and sucked hole, then squirted some over the towering column of Andrej's cock.

In the washed-out light of the moon, Grant gazed up into Andrej's eyes as the Croatian slowly impaled him with the entire length of his cock. The head was tapered and slid easily between his pouting asslips, while the shank that followed had more length than girth and found its way balls-deep with little effort.

"Oh yeah...so good! Thank you, Andrej," he murmured as he felt all that cock throbbing deep inside him and those balls nestling up against his crack.

"Thank you, Grant," Andrej murmured back.

He began a slow and rhythmic fuck. The deck moved with him as he leaned forward and placed a hand on either side of Grant's shoulders. They gazed at each other with absolute focus as cock slid in and out, slowly and steadily.

This was absolutely the best for Grant. Now he could feel the Croatian's slim body pressing against his own muscular one. The down-covered limbs were lean but firm, the cock in his ass a lengthy pole of relentless pumping action.

He reached up and wrapped his arms around Andrej, pulling him down and capturing his mouth with his own. They kissed again, open-mouthed and sloppy. Grant's hands explored the Croatian's lean back, then dropped down to cup and squeeze his marble-hard asscheeks. Unlike his usual passivity during sex, he began to push against those perfect cheeks, fucking himself with Andrej's cock.

The slow pump of cock in hole now became more emphatic and the boat rocked more erratically as Grant took over. Andrej moaned around Grant's tongue in his mouth while driving deep and then pulling out with his cock, faster and harder as the American's hands on his ass compelled him.

The rising tide of friction, for both asshole and cock, seemingly might have precipitated orgasm for either or both of them. But it didn't. Instead, they continued to fuck and kiss, neither ready or willing to release.

Grant wanted it to go on forever. His own cock was mashed between their bellies, slippery with lube from the copious squirting he'd done earlier. Andrej's firm belly pressed against it and rubbed it with maddening thoroughness. His asshole ached and throbbed and felt absolutely amazing. His knees in the air, he felt split in two, totally open to the Croatian's cock. His hands on the blond's firm ass pushed and pulled and kneaded.

Andrej seemed capable of fucking all night, his stiff cock plunging and withdrawing and plunging again. Fast, then slowing, fast again, until sweat oozed from both bodies in a slippery sheen that only increased the friction between their naked flesh.

It was Grant who surrendered first. He couldn't help it. Cock drove against his prostate in a relentless grind, propelled by his own shoving palms. His own cock oozed a steady stream of precum, then all at once began to swell with the inevitability of orgasm.

He couldn't stop it. Cum spewed. He broke their kiss and gasped out his capitulation. "I am so fucked! I'm coming, Andrej! I'm coming!"

It was the most incredible orgasm of his life. Andrej laughed breathlessly above him as he continued to pummel with his cock, every thrust eliciting another squirt of nut-cream between their bellies.

Only moments later, with Grant's asshole snapping around his driving cock, Andrej let go too. Shoving balls-deep, he came. He held himself inside Grant, filling the condom covering his spurting cock, pressing his belly against the pulsing release of Grant's cock.

They kissed again, enmeshed in sweaty heat, the rocking of the boat beneath them slowly settling.

Afterward they lay side by side and talked with the moon higher in the sky and their naked bodies awash in it. "I have shown you some of my country, and hope to show you more before you must leave us. And perhaps you can show me some of that boring country of Iowa afterward? Yes? But for now, please show me more of that exciting ass of yours!"

Grant rolled over onto his belly and Andrej placed a life preserver under his hips, then took his time exploring that husky butt with fingers, tongue and then cock. The second round lasted even longer than the first.

Grant fell asleep in Andrej's arms. The gentle rocking of the boat seemed to mimic their breathing and their shared heartbeat. He looked forward to dawn, and whatever it brought.

RIVER RAT

Josephine Myles

*M*y mother said / I never should / play with the gypsies in the wood...

I couldn't shake the old nursery rhyme as I walked along the towpath. I tried telling myself I wasn't in the bloody wood, this was the canal running through the middle of Manchester, and I'd probably end up getting clobbered if I mentioned the word *gypsy* when talking to the bloke. Not that I thought there was anything wrong with gypsies. I had a major hard-on for them, truth be told, but somehow I didn't reckon the redhead boater with the "fuck off" eyes was going to appreciate that label.

Even if he had called his boat *River Rat*.

His gaze had been dismissive the first time I clapped eyes on him, almost a fortnight ago. The sun had been making one of its rare appearances and he'd been shirtless, stripping down his engine on the towpath. I couldn't help staring at the grease mark across his tanned abs, wondering what his skin would taste like if I licked around it. I'd panned up to his face and realized I'd been rumbled. The moisture decided to desert my mouth like a rat from a sinking ship, and I almost went arse over tit stumbling into a pothole in the path as I scurried away. I might have been as tall as the boater, but I was a weedy art student, not a fighter, and wouldn't have stood a chance if he'd wanted to make something of it.

Of course, once I'd got back to my grotty shared house and locked myself in my room, I spent some quality time with my right hand, imagining what might have happened if he *had* decided to make something of it. This version involved sweaty naked wrestling, though, rather than the more realistic swift kick to the nuts and possible early watery grave. I conjured up the details I'd noticed in that brief glimpse of flesh: the brown nipples, the tufts of sweat-darkened ginger hair under his powerful arms, the rippling play of his muscles as he moved. I imagined being pinned down by him on the back deck of his narrowboat and taken without mercy. I came so fucking hard I swear I almost blacked out.

After that I took a stroll past his boat whenever I could fit it in around my classes. It wasn't far from campus, and I'd always used that stretch of towpath as a shortcut home, so I passed *River Rat* at least twice a day. I know it sounds desperate, but did I mention I had a kink for gypsies? It started when I was fifteen and just beginning to accept that this "fancying girls" thing probably wasn't ever going to kick in for me. The fair had been in town for the week, and my mates dragged me along saying all the fit birds would be there and we could probably buy some beer from the Pakistani guy who ran the corner shop, as rumor had it he'd accept the dodgiest of fake IDs.

Turned out it wasn't just rumor, and as I'd strolled along with my head pleasantly spinning, I realized I'd lost my mates to a gaggle of gum-chewing girls. I wandered over to the out-of-order

Ghost Train ride and spotted this carny leaning against the side, half-hidden behind the cheesily decorated façade. He was taking a break from tinkering with the generator and was smoking a roll-up. With his grease stained arms and bad-boy swagger, he definitely had that whole disreputable charm thing going on. My blood thundered to my dick as he ran a hot gaze up and down my body, and ten minutes later I was stumbling out of his caravan with an aching jaw and a bitter taste in my mouth.

Since that rough-and-ready blow job I'd fully embraced my sexuality (and a lot of other blokes along the way), but somehow that first experience had imprinted on me, and now whenever I caught a whiff of machine oil, all that excitement flooded back. I know, I know, I should just date a mechanic, but that wasn't enough. I wanted someone reckless and foot-loose. I wanted someone who stuck two fingers up at the establishment.

I wanted someone like my river rat.

I'd caught sight of him a couple more times, but he was always busy doing things to his engine and I don't think he noticed me checking him out—at best he'd give me a brief glare and get back to his work. Maybe he just thought I was staring at the boat. It was definitely eye-catching: jet black with the traditional signage on the side, the gleaming portholes and the array of knotted rope fenders on the roof that the hand-painted sign announced he made and sold. I could see some of them in action, hanging down the side of the boat to prevent it scraping against the concrete bank. I wondered if all that knotting had made his fingers deft and skillful, capable of wringing every last drop of pleasure from my body.

I wondered if I'd ever dare say anything to him. It would be easy if he sat out on the bank crafting his stupid bloody fenders because I could ask him something about that. I could pretend an artist's interest in handicrafts and engage him in conversation so he'd notice me. Remember me. Give me a fucking clue as to whether he was interested in other men.

But then last night I got my clue, and it was even more bloody frustrating. I was heading into one of the bars on Canal Street—one with a reputation for rough trade that I'd never dared venture into before—when I almost walked straight into him leaving the place. I could have kicked myself for spending so long getting ready, as he already had a tarty-looking goth boy hanging onto him. I shot the drunken twink a death-ray glare, but when I looked up to my river rat he just gave me this apologetic leer and raised his eyebrows before steering his prize off in the direction of his boat. I thought I heard him mutter "See you tomorrow," as they headed off, but I might have just been imagining things. I was so pissed off that even sucking off a huge biker in the toilets didn't do much to improve my mood, and his jizz could have tasted like the snakebite and black I'd been necking for all I noticed.

So anyway, there I was the next afternoon, walking along the towpath in my best pulling clothes, the painted-on jeans and black silk shirt, only marginally soiled from last night's escapade. I'd used as much hair putty as I thought I could get away with before turning into a hedgehog, and lined my eyes with enough kohl to make Marilyn Manson look restrained. I was hoping the smug twink wouldn't still be there, but if he was, I reckoned I could out-goth him any day.

Only problem was, I'd left my coat at home because the sun had been shining, but now a cold wind whipped out of nowhere and went right through me. I should know better, living in Manchester, but I'd selected my wardrobe using my little brain rather than the one best suited for forward planning. I hugged my arms tight around me as I stomped down the stretch of towpath toward his boat.

It wasn't there.

Just an empty stretch of bank, strewn with litter and crowned off with the most almighty pile of dog shit I've ever seen. As the first fat drops of rain hit my face, my eyes began to sting. Fucking typical. I was wearing cheap eye makeup that wasn't waterproof, and my favorite canvas shoes with the rainbow skulls on them were going to get soaked through. Seems the weather had it in for me, as rather than easing into a light splatter, the rain started bucketing down and I was soaked to the skin in moments.

"Fucking bastard!" I screamed up at the sky, although whether I was shouting at some imaginary deity or the absconded river rat, I have no idea.

"There you are. Thought I might find you hanging around. Come on, you're gonna get soaked."

I spun around to find him there behind me. The boater with the "fuck off" eyes. Except right now they weren't saying that at all; they were warm and he was close enough for me to see the amber flecks in the green. He wore a great big parka with one of those fur-lined hoods, which made me instantly jealous, even though you wouldn't catch me wearing one if it was the last item of clothing left in the world. I was too surprised to say anything, and he took hold of my arm with a firm grip and tutted, walking off and pulling me with him. I had to trot to keep up with his long strides.

"Come on, I've got the stove going and it's not far."

"Why'd you move?" I eventually remembered to ask him.

"Easier than cleaning up that pile of shit, wasn't it? Fucking arseholes, shouldn't be allowed to keep dogs if they don't clean up after them."

We headed under a bridge and the momentary shelter allowed me to rub my eyes, clearing them enough to see that familiar

black boat on the other side. Unfortunately, clearing my eyes led
to me getting huge smears of black over my hands. I looked like
I'd been sketching with charcoal. God knew what state my hair
was in. It felt like it had been plastered to my skull—not a good
look for someone as bony as me.

My rescuer didn't seem to mind, though. I chanced a quick
look at him, and he was squinting at me with a bemused smile.

"I'm Ryan, by the way," I blurted out. He kept staring. "And
this is the bit where you're meant to tell me your name."

"Does it matter?" He leered. "You'll get fucked whether you
know it or not."

"Oh. I, uh...no, I suppose not." I thought about it a moment.
"But I won't know whose name to shout when I'm coming."

He laughed at that and I caught sight of a gold tooth. "It's
Kev, but most people call me Ratty. On account of the boat,"
he added, which made me think he must have me down as a
moron. Mind you, since all I'd done up until now was gawk at
him, I suppose he didn't have much else to go on.

"I think I'd rather shout Kev, if it's all the same to you."

Kev chuckled, and then we were at his boat and he was pulling
me after him onto the *River Rat*'s front deck. There was barely
enough room for us both on there, and I had to fall against him
to avoid getting smacked in the chin when he opened the double
doors. I had a fleeting impression of hot, hard flesh under his
bulky coat before he pulled away to enter his home. I followed,
disoriented by the slight rock of the floor beneath me, the blast
of warm, coal-scented air, and the dim, coffin-like interior of
the *River Rat*.

But then Kev hit a light switch somewhere, and everything
leapt into warm tones, all rich wood and copper.

"Wow!" I couldn't help doing the open-mouthed moron
thing again, but Kev's boat wasn't like any home I'd ever been

into before. I was standing in what must be the living room, as
there was a low sofa covered in a rich red throw along one side,
the stove on the other. A huge pile of those fender things he sold
was placed where it could make a perfect footrest, a coil of fine
rope crowning the heap. It felt extra cozy with the rain drumming loudly on the roof and running over the portholes.

"So, you gonna let all my hot air out or what?"

I mumbled an apology as I shut the doors behind me and
fumbled with the latch. Eventually I got the bloody thing
fastened, and turned around to find Kev grinning at me from
behind what must be a kitchen counter, judging by all the uten-
sils swaying from hooks on the ceiling.

"You want to get straight to the fucking, or would you like
a cup of tea first?"

What a choice! I was going to opt for fucking first, because the
very mention of it had my prick perking up, but then a massive
sneeze ripped through me and I stumbled to sit on the sofa.

"Better make it a brandy by the sound of it. Here."

I took the mug, which had a good inch or so of the stuff in it,
and downed it as fast as I could. Having Kev standing there in
front of me was definitely helping to warm me up. My jeans were
literally steaming. Mind you, that might have been due to the
stove, which was kicking out heat like nobody's business.

I handed the mug back and looked up at him. His eyes
glowed in the watery light spilling through the portholes, and I
figured he was waiting for me to make a move. I leaned forward
to bury my face in his crotch. He was wearing urban camou-
flage combat trousers, and I mouthed the thick shaft of his prick
through the fabric.

I felt the weight of his hand on my head, and then a surprised
sound. "You're drenched, aren't you? I'm getting you a towel.
You'd better strip those wet things off."

And so there I was, ten minutes later, sitting dressed in nothing more than a threadbare towel, with a mug of brandy-scented tea in my hands. This seduction thing wasn't really going to plan: I might be naked, but there wasn't any action happening. No, instead, Kev was treating me to a rundown of how he knotted the ropes to make those bloody boat fenders. I'm not into handicrafts—they're just fine art's dowdy cousins—hicks from the country. But then I got to thinking about this website I'd found with pictures of guys all tied up in a decorative way. Something Japanese, I recalled, and struggled to remember the name.

"Shibari!" I exclaimed, interrupting Kev's demonstration of a knot.

He raised his eyebrows and gave me this long, assessing stare. I brazened it out.

"Are you trying to tell me you want to be tied up?" Kev asked, his voice sounding rougher than it had a moment ago.

"Do you know how?" I licked my lips and shifted so that the towel fell open, revealing a slice of pale thigh. Kev's gaze tracked down, and his eyes turned dark as a nightclub ceiling.

"Hang on a second. Don't want to give any passersby a free show." Kev flicked a brass switch on the wall behind him and we were plunged into the gloom again, lit only by dull daylight filtering through the portholes. But it was enough to see Kev pick up the coil of rope and run it through his hands.

"This isn't the right sort of rope. It's gonna hurt you."

"I don't care."

"Yeah, but maybe I do." Kev's voice got soft there, making me think wild and unlikely things I quickly shoved to the back of my mind. This was just a one-off hookup. No point hoping for anything more.

"Besides," Kev said, straddling me on the sofa, then leaning in to speak in a low rumble against my neck, "I don't think you should go about letting strange men tie you up. You could get into all kinds of trouble."

He emphasized the last word with a squeeze to my dick that made me gasp and buck up into his hand.

"I mean," Kev continued, rough stubble rasping my neck, "I could tie you and gag you, then cruise off and no one would have any idea where you were. I could keep you here as my slave and fuck you whenever I wanted."

I groaned, his words making my heart pound and my dick throb along with it.

"Oh, you'd like that, would you?"

"Yeah," I managed to pant out. "So long as you let me out to go to college. Don't wanna fuck it all up this close to graduation."

Kev laughed against my neck, rubbing my skin deliciously sore. I wanted him to use me and spread me and fuck me raw. I raised my hands up above my head and clung on to the brass light fixture.

Kev sat back up and looked at me again, his gaze burrowing right into me and pulling out all my secret desires and kinks.

"Tell me what you want, Ryan."

"I want you to fuck my mouth." It wasn't everything I wanted, but it would certainly do for now.

Kev nodded once, then stood and stripped off his boots and trousers. He went commando, which I'd somehow expected, but I wasn't anticipating how white he'd be. There was a stark line at his belt where the freckled bronze of his upper body gave way to ivory skin, only slightly darkened by the fuzz of his coppery hair. But then I lost concentration as he was kneeling over me again, but this time with his hand pressing down on my head and his ruddy cock pushing against my lips.

I opened wide for him, drooling as he thrust inside, shallow strokes quickly giving way to deep plunges. I felt my jaw begin to ache and my throat bruise as he used me. It was fucking perfect, me clinging onto the light fixture and choking on his thick, meaty dick, and him forcing his way in with a grunt. I gasped for air whenever I could, but kept up the suction and tried not to whimper too pathetically when he slammed into the back of my throat.

My nuts were threatening to burst by the time he pulled out, and I stared down at my neglected cock. It dribbled some precome as I watched. I lowered one of my hands, thinking to give it a little attention, and felt my arm muscles scream in protest. And then a hand locked around my wrist like a manacle.

"No, you don't." Kev's voice sounded hoarse, but the tone of command was unmistakable. It prompted even more blood to rush to the party in my dick.

"On your knees," Kev ordered, releasing his hold on my wrist. "Face-down. Yeah, that's it. You've got such a tight. Fuckable. Little. Arse." He punctuated the last words with dry finger thrusts inside me. I didn't know whether I wanted to pull away from the pain or push back into it. It felt like he had at least two fingers in me; they were thick and calloused, catching my rim with a sharp sting every time he pumped in and out. I sobbed with frustration, until the burn gave way to sharp pleasure.

"Yeah, that's right. Ride my fingers."

I did so gladly, despite the friction of his rough skin. I knew I'd be feeling this for days, and the thought made me moan. But just as the sensations threatened to send me over the edge again, Kev pulled out. I heard cursing behind me, felt the boat sway as Kev stomped around, but I kept my forehead buried against the sofa cushion, panting in an effort to calm my body's responses. I know I hadn't been specifically told not to, but I doubted Kev would approve if I shot my load before he'd had a chance to shove his dick in me.

"There's the buggers! Thought that little bitch might have stolen my supplies. He was a sly one. Not much of a shag, either. Should have ditched him when I saw you, shouldn't I?"

"Yeah, you should have," I rasped, the memory of Kev and the twink walking past me doing wonders at chasing away my immanent orgasm. But then I realized what Kev was saying, and a surge of joy put me right back where I had been. I pushed my arse up higher, praying like fuck Kev would hurry up and just do me.

Moments later, there was the unmistakable sensation of a fat, lubed prick pressing against me and demanding entrance. All other thoughts flew out the porthole as he plowed into me. Kev pushed against my resisting muscles and they gave way with a bright pain.

"Shit!" I whimpered and writhed but he kept on coming, and then I was stuffed to the gills. I swear, he'd thrust so far inside me I could feel him at the back of my throat. I was gloriously impaled and I fucking loved it. Kev's fingers explored around my stretched skin and he made approving noises.

"Wish you could see this. You look bloody gorgeous with me in you."

"Take a picture. It'll last longer." And just get on with it, I wanted to say, but didn't dare.

"Yeah, next time. Camera's all the way over there."

And then Kev gripped my hips and started to draw out, a long stroke that almost had him pulling free before plunging back in again and forcing the air out of my lungs. I had to brace my hands against the sofa cushion, clinging on as best I could as he slammed into me again and again. I tried to join in, tried to move back against him, but it was all I could do just to breathe and keep from being pushed flat onto my stomach. His balls slapped into mine so hard it stung, but that only seemed to make them more intent on shooting their load.

"Need to get deeper," Kev panted before lifting one of my legs and forcing my knee up toward my shoulder. I was spread wide, and I arched my back as he pushed in even deeper than he had before. He ground his hips against me, the rough bush of his pubes rubbing against my sweaty skin. The change of angle meant he pushed right into that knot of nerves, and bursts of energy zinged down to my balls and out through my dick. I rolled my forehead against the sofa, aware of nothing more than the pounding I was getting and the soundtrack of the rain on the roof and Kev's staccato grunts.

And then there was a rough hand squeezing my dick, and I came on the second pump, bliss sweeping through me like a flash flood. Kev fucked me through it, hard and fast, then stiffened and yelled.

When I came to, strong arms were pulling me off the wet patch, and that towel reappeared. I slumped against Kev and his arm pulled me close. That was nice. I hated getting the brush-off straight after sex.

"Sorry," I said eventually.

"Hmm? What for? You're a great shag. Sen-bloody-sational."

I grinned at that. "I forgot to shout your name when I came. I was kinda distracted, what with the way you were shafting me."

"Next time."

"Aren't you going to be moving on soon?" I knew there was some regulation that kept the boaters moving every couple of weeks.

"Yeah, but only to the marina. I've got a spot there booked

from the first of next month. Felt like staying somewhere busy for a while. Gets a bit lonely sometimes, out there in the countryside."

I pouted. "So you're not going to tie me up and take me away from all this?"

Kev chuckled, and his lips moved against my ear.

"Nope, but I'll tell you what I will do. Tomorrow I'm going to go out and buy a length of special rope, and then I'm going to get you back here and start a new hobby."

"Sounds like fun." I yawned and settled down against his warm body, the drumming of the raindrops lulling me into sweet dreams of being trussed up and shafted.

That's a handicraft I could definitely get into.

SHANGHAI
SURPRISE

Rob Rosen

The bar looked clean enough, I suppose. Hell, cleaner than any of the rest of them Barbary Coast pubs I poked my head into that night. I mean, I finally had me some coins to rub together, I did. Enough to buy me some whiskey with, maybe even get me a decent meal. I reckoned I worked hard enough for it, deserved something better than just a watered-down beer and some fried pig fat, which was about all I'd been living on since I arrived in San Francisco a couple of weeks earlier.

See, all I needed was some money first. Enough to buy me a few tools and a ride on out to the gold. Least that's what I was planning on. Not what I got, though. Nope, not by a fucking long shot. Got me a whole mess of trouble instead. And it all started with the likes of him.

Feller walked into the bar just after I did. Heck, I didn't even have a chance to order me up some grub. Was about to when he up and walks over. "This seat taken?" he asked, that brogue of his as thick as molasses, eyes as green as a field of clover, his mane of red hair swirling atop his head and below his chin like he was on fire or something.

"Nope," I said to him, with a polite nod. "Help yourself."

He pulled up a stool and threw down a leather satchel, his eyes locking with mine, grinning so bright that the sun got all of a sudden jealous. "Had me a fine day today, laddie," he said to me. "Oh, a mighty fine day indeed."

"That right?" I asked, my knee bouncing all nervous-like. "Why's that, stranger?"

He looked around, eyes in a squint, then he up and dumps the contents of the pouch onto the table. The coins came clattering down, gold glinting in the meager light of the bar. He covered them up right quick and whispered to me, "Good day in the mines, laddie. Found me a nugget the size of me eyeball, I did."

I gulped, my own eyeballs wide now. See, I'd heard the stories, I did. Men striking it rich like that. Heck, them stories is what brought me out to California in the first place. Now here I was, face-to-face with a living, breathing example of it. "Congrats, stranger," I said to him, trying to keep my voice from breaking.

He nodded and slid the coins back inside their pouch. "Jack," he said, his hand held out.

"Ben," I told him, with a firm shake. "Ben Beauregard. Pleased to meet you."

His grip lingered, eyes boring deep on down. Then he smiled at me again, a swarm of butterflies suddenly set loose in my belly. "Drinks are on me, Ben," he said. "Dinner, too, if'n you're hungry. Heck, I s'pose I could buy this whole bar if I wanted to now."

I smiled back at him, glad at least that someone had struck it rich. Maybe his good fortune would wear off on me. I settled for a tall glass of whiskey and bowl of stew, all on him, just as he'd said. Minutes later, he plunked it all down and joined me, his snifter filled to the brim, our meals steaming on up to the rafters. "Thanks," I said, hungrily eyeing my first good meal in weeks.

"Dig in, laddie," he told me, eyes twinkling like the stars up in the sky, red beard dripping off of him like a river of blood.

So that's just what I did. Ate it all like a man who hadn't eaten in days. Which wasn't too far from the truth. Drank down the whiskey, too, and then had me another one, Jack watching me with that ever-present grin of his as I did so. Only, right away, it wasn't sitting too good with me. Had me a pang, all of sudden. "Uh," I groaned, hand clutching at my side, the pain ricocheting through me, like a hornet had suddenly got loose in there.

"What's the matter, laddie? Done ate too fast, did ya?" he asked, leaning in, looking to me like the cat that done just ate the canary.

And then the room started spinning like a twister and the lights went low on me. I seem to recall trying to stand, only my legs buckled and I teetered forward. Then that dim light closed in, black going even blacker, and all I could hear was a storm of laughter, wave after wave of it crashing down over on me, dragging me under.

When I opened my eyes again, the waves were still there, except they were real, honest-to-goodness ones now. And I wasn't in the bar no more. And, damn, if my head didn't feel like it'd been split open in two. I tried to stand, only I got pulled back. "Shackles," I coughed out, staring down at my feet, the rusted metal clamped down tight around my ankles. "What the hell?" I managed, just as I heard the footsteps up above, then on the stairs off to my side.

"Ah, you're up now, laddie. About damn time, too."

"Jack," I said, my throat dry as a desert. "Where...where are we?"

He grinned, shrugged. "Oh, I'd say about an hour up the coast already."

And then I knew what'd happened. "Shanghaied," I coughed out.

He nodded. "That's what they call it, laddie. Though that ain't where it is you're headed. Shanghai, I mean. See, that there gold rush you came out for, it done sucked up all the able-bodied men in these here parts, it did. Not enough sailors left for whaling."

I yanked on my chains and stifled back a sob. "But I don't know anything about whaling, Jack."

He laughed and crouched down, eye to eye with me once again. "Laddie, you didn't know nothing about gold neither, but that didn't stop you none, now did it?" He slapped my knee and nodded. "Besides, what's there to know? All you'll be doing is rowing. After I drop you off in Portland, I mean."

"Then...then what?"

Again he shrugged. "Hell if I know. Alaska, I s'pose. I just get me my money bringing men such as yourself to the boats. After that, well, like I said, hell if I know." He laughed and patted my shoulder. "But you'll get paid, laddie. Probably make you more money than most of them men is making out in the mines. See, only the rich is getting richer when it comes to the gold. Men like you is getting nothing but sorrow, they is."

I rattled the chains and squinted my eyes at him. "Sorrow I done already know about, Jack," I said to him. "Got me it in spades."

He reached across the gap and tousled my hair. "That's life, laddie." Then he fiddled inside his back pocket and lifted out a key. "You ever sail before, Ben?"

I shook my head no. "Never even seen the ocean until just recently. Wish I never had."

He chuckled. "Well then, guess I can unchain you. I mean, since you can't sail this old girl, you ain't about to go trying nothing funny now, will ya?"

I rubbed my ankles, which were nicked and bloodied. "I reckon not, Jack. I reckon not." I snickered, despite the circumstances. "But maybe you should sleep with one eye open, just in case."

His shrug returned and the key got twisted inside the lock. "Good to know, Ben. One eye open it is, then." The shackles fell off and clattered down onto the wood below. I sighed and again rubbed my ankles, the skin now purple and bruised, before Jack stood up and helped me to my feet. I rocked right along with that boat of his, landing with a thud against his chest. "Don't you worry none, laddie; you'll be getting your sea legs soon enough," he told me, his breath hot on my chin as those butterflies in my belly took flight again.

"I think I'm gonna be sick," I moaned, holding on good and tight to him, his muscles like heavy rocks beneath my hands.

He grinned and led me up the stairs. "Do it over the side of the boat, Ben, 'cause I ain't about to clean up after ya."

I ran to the side and leaned over, the sea below churning, darker than the midnight sky. I heaved and upchucked, the apparently spiked stew and whiskey spilling out of my guts before disappearing into the swirling water, which rocked and shook the boat beneath my feet. I puked again, until my stomach was empty and my throat was burning, the tears streaming down my cheeks like a rainstorm.

"I hate you, Jack," I coughed out.

He laughed and came over, patting my back. "That's what they all say, Ben. Now go sit aft with ya and keep out of my way."

So I stumbled to the rear of the boat and slunk down on

my butt to the cold wood floor, willing my stomach to keep quiet and my head to stop spinning. I focused on Jack instead, watching him maneuver the ship, yanking on ropes, swinging the sail over our heads, the material catching the strong ocean breeze before sending us speeding through the water, fast as lightning. All the while, the muscles in his hair-dense forearms bulged and flexed, as did his chest from beneath his cotton shirt, the red curly hairs poking out from beneath the collar.

I sat there, transfixed. In truth, I'd never seen a man like Jack before. It was like him and that ship of his were attached somehow. He seemed to know every inch of her, every creak and groan, knew what to shift and pull and push on a split second before it needed to be done, all while the sea tossed around us, spraying the both of us in a salty mist. Made my heart pound just watching him, it did. Made my prick pretty much do the same. See, it wasn't just a good meal I hadn't had in weeks.

Sadly, my heart wasn't about to stop pounding for quite some time to come. Not once those gray clouds rolled in, the thunder booming overhead as the sky went dark in nearly the blink of an eye. "Hold on!" he hollered over at me, his fiery hair whipping in the breeze.

I grabbed on to the nearby bench just as the sky cracked open and a flood came pouring on down, both of us drenched in an instant. The sail caught a sudden gust of wind and took us into a wall of water, the boat groaning, ready, it seemed, to break apart beneath us. But still Jack steered her, trying as best as he could to keep her steady, his face locked in a grimace, body tensed up tight, eyes burning bright. "Untie the sail, laddie!" he shouted, his voice barely breaking through the din of the sudden storm.

I hopped up and nearly fell right the hell on over, the boat pitching me this way and that. Still, I made it to the ropes, managing to untie the knots he'd made, and watched as the sail came crashing down around us. The boat, at last, slowed down just a bit, riding with the waves instead of crashing headlong into them.

"Now what?" I hollered over at him.

He stared up at the sky, hands like a vise on the wheel, a vein throbbing in his neck as that mane of red flew to the side. "Wait it out, laddie!" he yelled up to the heavens. "See who breaks first, it or us!" And then he laughed, the rain flicking this way and that off of him. "Hope you're not a betting man, Ben," he added. "Because the odds ain't too good right about now!"

I lurched forward and grabbed on to the wheel, standing side by side with him as the rain came down in buckets. "Then let's see about evening them up a bit, Jack!" I shouted, helping him as best I could to keep the boat stable.

He sidled in next to me, shoulder to shoulder. "Keep her steady as she goes, laddie!" he shouted into the wind, the boat crashing into the waves. "Steady as she goes!"

And steady is what we kept her, our feet rooted to the deck, hands locked onto the wheel, side by side, wave after wave after endless wave hitting us as the sky went from gray to black and back again. Never felt so damned cold and soaked through in all my years, every bone in my body ready to crack and give way, moaning as fiercely as that ship of his.

Then, hours later, the last miserable drop hit the top of the mast just as the sky began turning red, red as his dripping beard, in fact. He turned and looked at me. "Made it through, laddie," he managed, with a crooked grin, his head at a tilt as he stared at me. "You's shaking like a leaf, Ben. Best get you into some dry clothes before you catch your death up here. Then you won't be worth a plugged nickel to me."

I looked out at the ocean, the waves at last barely breaking, and I finally exhaled. Seemed like I'd been holding my breath all that time, almost. I released my grip, fingers aching, back aching, legs aching. "G-good i-dea," I replied, teeth chattering as I fought with my body to follow him.

Back down below, he tossed me a change of clothes and grabbed some for himself, a thin towel for the both of us added to the pile. Though, by then, we needed a good half a dozen. Then I watched him undress, one soaking-wet piece of clothing after the next removed, freckled skin exposed, rife with muscle, scars, red hair that caught the water like moss after a rain. Until he and I were naked, both of us shaking, his dangling cock swaying back and forth.

He grabbed the towel and moved on over to me, cradling my head in it, giving it a rubdown before moving it around my shoulders, my back, my chest, which was rising and falling in a steady rhythm with the ocean. Still he kept going, down my back, around my legs and, lastly, over my prick, staring up at me as he tried his best to dry me off. "Better?" he asked, moving his hand away.

I stared down, my cock beginning a slow arc up. Damned thing had a mind of its own, sometimes. A hot flush of red rose up my neck. "Uh, looks that way, I reckon."

He stood up, and my eyes went wide. His own hooded tool was standing as ramrod straight as the mast above, the piss slit winking at me within the quickly unfolding flesh, revealing the wide helmeted head within. "Guess they's happy to be alive, laddie," he said, his voice suddenly thick, coarse.

"Them and me both," I agreed, tentatively reaching out to grab the happy beast, with Jack moaning in response, eyes rolling on back inside his head.

When he opened them back up, he was smiling from ear to ear, his hand reaching out to grab my prick, both of them getting jerked now. "But you're still shaking, laddie. Ya need some warmth in you, and quick."

He closed the gap between us, wrapped his thick arms around me, getting us chest to chest, cocks ground up tight together as his hands rubbed my back. My own hands landed on his ass, which was fairly covered in fuzzy down, my chin now resting on his shoulder. The two of us stood there like that for quite some time, too, getting gently rocked back and forth, until my body warmed up a few degrees and my quaking finally stopped.

I looked up at him, into those fields of green, his smile ever-present. See, I ain't never kissed a man before, but it sure seemed like a good idea right about then. I reckon he thought so, too, because his lips were on mine soon enough, mashing together, both of us swapping some heavy spit as my fingers went from his cheeks on in to the crinkled center.

"Whatcha doin' back there, laddie?" he asked, grinning, once he came up for air.

"Little trick I done learned back East," I replied with a wink. "Care to see it?"

My wink got volleyed back. "I'm game." He backed an inch away and we looked down at our rock-hard cocks, which were dripping something fierce by then. "Looks like they're game, as well."

He walked me over to his bunk and hopped on in, body prone, splayed out before me. Was a beautiful sight to see, too. "You're a fine-looking man, Jack," I managed, getting in there with him, my body again on his, lips pressed up so snug it was impossible to tell where I ended and he began. "Bet you taste just as good," I added, soon enough.

"Only one way to tell, laddie," he whispered in my ear before taking a gnash on a tender lobe.

I moaned and eagerly began my move down him, my chin

making its way through a field of red chest hair, across his peaks and valleys, kissing and nibbling my way to his prick, which stood at rapt attention, waiting patiently for me in the center of it all. See, I might not have kissed a man before, but I sure as hell sucked me some cock in my day. Only, maybe none quite as big as Jack's.

Over and down my mouth went, spunk hitting the back of my throat like a bullet as I managed as much of his meat as I could, a gagging tear dripping down my cheek. For his part, Jack moaned and groaned and pushed down on my head with his mighty grip. "Aye, laddie, suck that log of mine."

And so I did, sucking and jacking it, all the while yanking and twisting his heavy, hairy nuts, until I had his back arched up and off the cot, his groans bouncing around all that wood that surrounded us. Then my mouth went south, licking its way down the length of his massive tool, lapping its way across and around his balls, which I sucked on with abandon.

Only, I wasn't done just yet. Not by a mile, I wasn't. I done lifted his legs up and out, his puckered hole coming into view, haloed in a ring of fire-red hair, winking out at me all come-hither like. The rain had washed him out clean as a whistle, with my tongue happily finishing the job. Eagerly, I dove on in, sucking that pretty asshole of his for all it was worth, licking and lapping at it before I glided my tongue inside, all while he jacked his cock, balls banging my forehead, his body thrashing atop the creaking cot.

"Better fill her up, laddie," he grunted, "before I blow."

Seeing as my own cock was getting jacked to just before blowing, I jumped up onto my knees, spat on his hole and my prick, and then teased my head inside him. All of a sudden, my body sizzled, a spark riding up my spine as I slid it on home. My face tilted back, mouth in a pant, as his asshole gripped at my cock, sucking it in deeper, until my balls were banging up against his rump.

I stared down at him, him up at me, his fist working fast on that giant club of his, muscles so tense you could see them etched across his body. "Aye now, laddie, fuck me hard," he rasped.

"Gladly, Jack," I groaned, ramming my cock deep inside his ass before yanking it out and then shoving it in again, out and in, out and in, pummeling his hole but good, my bones no longer cold and aching but on fire now, sweat pouring down my body in a mighty stream. Then I was so deep up in him that I nearly cracked him in two.

"Fuuuck," he groaned, the sound traveling down his body and up into mine, just as that giant pecker of his shot and shot and shot, one thick band of come after the next, rising high up in the air before it came splashing down on his chest and belly.

"Fuuuck," I echoed, a giant wad of come filling him up before seeping out his hole and dripping down to the cot below, my body twitching, butt grinding as I came and came and came some more.

Panting now, I popped my prick out of his ass and collapsed on top of him, our mouths again finding each other, tongues snaking and coiling, hands roaming, all with that sticky man-sap of his covering us both. Exhausted, I soon rolled off and spooned him from the side, my cheek on his shoulder, finger plucking at one of his thick nipples, my body fully relaxed at long last.

Guess I fell asleep like that, too, because when I woke up, he was gone. It was just me and the cot, both of us sticky with dried come. I started to rise, but heard a voice up above, then two. It was Jack and another man. I waited, realizing we weren't moving anymore, just rocking in place. My heart started to beat fast all of a sudden. This was it, I realized. Time for the swap. Me for the coins; my life never the same again.

"Where is he?" asked the stranger.

"Gone," said Jack as I sucked in my breath. "Lost in the storm."

The other man laughed. "Guess you came up here for nothing then, Jack."

Jack laughed, too. I pictured his head titled back, wild mess of hair flying in the breeze. "Well now, I wouldn't say that."

I sat up as they walked above me, until only one of the men was left. Then I listened as the feet came charging down. "What are you doing just lounging there, laddie? Be quick about you."

I sat up, legs dangling off the side of the cot, and stared at him, unsure of what to do next. Had I been sold or not? "Quick about what, Jack?" I asked, voice nearly catching in my throat.

He moved in and crouched in front of me, hands on my thighs, green eyes sparkling like emeralds. "First-mate duties, laddie," he said, with a wink. "Gotta teach you how to work this old girl, so that the next storm won't be as bad for us."

"The next one, huh?" I said, bending down to brush my lips against his, his beard now dry and tickling my chin.

He gripped my cock, which was already rising and growing thick. "Aye," he said, leaning in to slap it against his mouth. "The next one, and the one after that and the one after that." He looked up at me, his tongue licking off the sticky jizz from the tip of my prick. "Guess I've been out here alone long enough. I s'pose I could use me some help."

I chuckled and slid my steely cock inside his opened mouth. "Looks like I struck gold, after all, Jack," I moaned, hands running through that fiery mane of his. "And a mighty thick vein of it, too."

SAILING LESSONS

Aaron Michaels

The boat was going to capsize.

T.J. kicked his feet to keep his head above water. The life jacket did a good enough job, just like it was supposed to, but the late-afternoon wind made the water on the lake choppy. He didn't mind playing the helpless man overboard—it was all part of Uncle Raymond's sailing lesson and T.J. was a pretty good swimmer—but he was sure the lesson wasn't supposed to include capsizing the damn sailboat. All his uncle was supposed to do was turn the boat around and bring it back to pick up T.J. He wasn't supposed to turn it so sharply that the wind caught the sail wrong and blew the whole thing over.

I'm never going to hear the end of this, T.J. thought as he watched Raymond slide into the water as the boat rolled over on its side. At least the float on top of the single mast would keep the boat from turning completely upside down, and the instructor was on board to help Raymond right the thing, but the look of pure horror on Raymond's face said volumes. The lesson was over.

All T.J. had wanted to do was give his uncle a nice birthday present. Raymond had always said he'd wanted to learn how to sail. Ever since Aunt Gladdie had taken up with a man half her (and Raymond's) age, T.J.'s uncle had done little except sit around the house. Fifty-two was too young to crawl into a cave and mope, so T.J. had purchased—at no small expense, mind you—sailing lessons for his uncle. Raymond had insisted that the only proper way to thank T.J. was to bring him along on what was supposed to be the last lesson in the series, since Raymond needed a volunteer to pretend to fall off the boat. T.J. figured he'd have an easy afternoon at the lake. An added bonus was discovering the sailboat instructor was pretty easy on the eyes.

The safety boat motored up next to T.J. "You need a hand?" yelled the young woman at the rail.

"Give me a minute," T.J. yelled back.

He really wanted to give his uncle a chance to finish the lesson, but it didn't look like that was going to happen. The sailboat was small enough that one person could right it, but Raymond wasn't even trying. He knew how—that had been the subject of an earlier lesson, the instructor had said, one T.J. hadn't come along for—but now Raymond was just hanging on to the stern while the instructor worked to bring the boat upright.

Once the sail was out of the water, it was just a matter of counterbalance. The instructor climbed over the side and into the boat as the sail straightened, and the boat suddenly looked like a sailboat again instead of the victim of a tropical storm.

Of course, the instructor no doubt had tons of practice rescuing sailboats. He was a long, lean man in his late twenties, just like T.J., only where T.J. was fair, the instructor, whose name was Rick, was olive-skinned and dark-haired with an easy smile, a face that could have graced a fashion catalog, and a body that looked great in a cut-off wetsuit. He had the kind of natural athleticism that some guys were just born with. T.J. wasn't in bad shape himself, but he had to work at it. Rick made righting the boat look easy. T.J. wondered what else Rick might make look easy, just like he'd spent half the lesson wondering what Rick would look like with his wetsuit off.

Even with the instructor on board, T.J.'s uncle still was making no move to hoist himself back on board and come rescue T.J.

Yup, the lesson was over.

"Guess I do need rescuing," T.J. yelled at the young woman waiting at the rail.

The safety boat was the only motored boat allowed on the lake. Technically, it wasn't really a lake, only a man-made marina created at the site of a former rock quarry. Small enough for an easy walk around the circumference but large enough to get a sailboat going a decent speed in the right wind, it was the only place in town to get sailing lessons. When T.J. had called for information, the staff at the marina had assured him that the lessons were perfectly safe, right down to the motorboat that shadowed the sailboats.

The man piloting the safety boat pulled it in front of T.J. so he could reach the float at the back. T.J. pulled himself out of the water and climbed aboard. The man looked over his shoulder. "Need a towel?" he asked.

T.J. shook his head. It was August and hot. The cold lake water had felt good.

"I don't think your friend's having a good time," the woman said, nodding at where Rick, the instructor, was hauling Raymond out of the water.

"My uncle," T.J. said automatically. "And you're right, he isn't." So much for Raymond's dream of being a sailor. "I thought this would be fun for him."

"It still might be. This is his last lesson, right?"

T.J. nodded.

"Look at it this way." She nodded at the sailboat. Raymond was sitting in the stern, his shoulders slumped, while Rick worked the sail. "Your uncle made it this far. A lot of people think sailing looks like fun. They take a lesson, realize it can be hard work, and they quit. He didn't. Give him some credit. He's not as young or in as good shape as you are."

She said the last with a smile, and T.J. realized she was flirting with him. Why couldn't it be the sexy sailing instructor doing the flirting? Then again, the guy was probably straight. T.J. hadn't done any serious dating in so long, he was bound to have fantasies about any reasonably hot guy in a wetsuit, straight or not.

And now it looked like he wouldn't even have the opportunity to watch Rick up close for the rest of the lesson. Instead of piloting the sailboat over so that T.J. could get back on board, the sailboat was heading back for the docks.

Leaving T.J. behind.

"Wow," he said. "Guess I really do need rescuing. Can you give me a lift back to my car?"

The woman's smile got bigger. "We have to stay on the lake until everyone's headed back, but sure, you can hang out with us."

Three other sailboats were on the lake. T.J. caught the guy at the wheel giving him a sympathetic look. Either the guy knew T.J. was gay, or more likely the woman was a serial flirter.

"You know what?" T.J. said to her. "I could really use a towel after all."

He sat down on a bench seat while the woman retrieved a towel from a cabinet beneath the wheel.

It was going to be a long afternoon.

* * *

Uncle Raymond was nowhere to be found when T.J. finally made it back to the dock. Raymond hadn't been waiting on the dock, so T.J. thought he might be drowning his sorrows at the bar in the dockside restaurant that overlooked the water, but he was gone.

And so was T.J.'s car.

What the hell?

They'd left their street clothes along with wallets, keys and cell phones in the same locker in the gym in a little row of shops next to the marina office. Raymond's clothes—both street and wet boating clothes—and his phone were gone, along with T.J.'s car keys.

T.J. dialed Raymond's cell phone. The call went right to voice mail.

"You took my car?" T.J. said. "It's one thing to leave me stranded on the lake, but to take my car? I can't believe you did that!" He made himself take a deep breath. "Look, call me, okay?" He disconnected the call. He probably shouldn't talk to his uncle that way, but really. What kind of uncle swipes his nephew's car?

"Having problems?"

T.J. turned around. Rick, the sailboat instructor, was standing behind him. He'd changed out of his wetsuit into cream-colored linen pants and a Hawaiian shirt. His hair was wet, but he smelled like shampoo, not lake water.

T.J. was suddenly aware that he hadn't showered yet and probably didn't smell all that good. "Uh, yeah." He nodded toward the parking lot in front of the gym. "My uncle left me stranded."

Rick's eyes widened. "That was your car?" He shook his head. "Man, that takes balls."

"Tell me about it." T.J. had the money for a cab ride, but nobody who owned a car liked taking a cab. Not in their own hometown, especially not sober. Cab rides were for getting your drunken, bar-crawling butt home after a night out with friends.

"I saw him head out to the car," Rick said, "but I figured you just met up here. If I'd have known..." He shrugged.

"Don't worry about it. Shit happens."

T.J. really needed to shower off, but this was the longest conversation he'd had with Rick without his uncle around, and if he hadn't been so annoyed about his car, he might actually be enjoying himself.

Ah, well. Probably for the best. The guy no doubt had a gorgeous girlfriend at home.

"Let me buy you a drink," Rick said.

T.J. blinked. Had he heard that right?

"You really look like you could use one, and if you're taking a cab anyway..." Rick nodded toward the restaurant. "It's the end of my day, and I usually hit happy hour before I go home. They have pretty good fried clams if you're into that sort of thing."

The restaurant had a seafood theme, so the fried clams weren't all that surprising. The invitation for a drink was.

"Okay," T.J. said, still wondering if this was just a let's-be-chums drink.

Rick's eyes drifted lower for a moment, then back up to T.J.'s face. *Well, hello.* T.J. guessed he had his answer.

"You might want to shower first, though. You'd be more comfortable," Rick said.

T.J. grinned, his uncle's behavior pretty much forgotten. "Won't take me long," he said.

"See you soon," Rick said, grinning back.

The water in the shower was hot. T.J. had a momentary vision of Rick stripping off and joining him, but of course, that didn't happen. Those type of things only happened in movies, and bad ones at that. The men's locker room at the gym was too public. All the sailing lessons might be done for the day, but there were a few guys still working out in the gym. The shower stalls weren't all that private.

After T.J. finished off his shower with a blast of cold water and changed into his street clothes, he called his uncle one more time. The call went to voice mail. Again. This time he didn't leave a message.

T.J. was surprised to find Rick was waiting for him in the gym. He'd thought they were going to meet up at the bar. He'd planned on using the short walk from the gym to the bar to think up conversation starters. He hadn't been on a date in a long time. All he knew about Rick was that the guy gave sailing lessons. What else would they talk about?

He needn't have worried. It turned out that conversation came as easy to Rick as his smile.

"Your uncle's a pretty cool guy," Rick said. "Well, when he's not driving off in a car that doesn't belong to him, but otherwise, from what I saw, he's not bad for a guy whose life's turned upside down."

"You know about that?" T.J. didn't think his uncle talked to anyone about what Aunt Gladdie had done.

"Guys his age, they come out for lessons for a couple of reasons. One—they're having a delayed midlife crisis, and it's a sailboat instead of a red convertible."

T.J. couldn't imagine his uncle in a convertible. The man drove a ten-year-old Lincoln.

"Two," Rick said. "They're retired and want something to do with their time besides gardening and golf."

Raymond had never shown any interest in golf.

"Or three—someone gave them a present because they thought the guy could use some cheering up."

T.J. felt his cheeks flush. "That would be me, and he did. But I only did it because when I was little, he always told me that someday he wanted to sail."

"He told me about that, too," Rick said. "Let's see if I've got this straight. He used to take you to the park so you could play with toy boats on this little pond. One day this bigger kid and his dad came along with one of those remote-controlled motorized boats, and the wake knocked your sailboat over. Your uncle told you not to worry."

"That a sailboat was more elegant," T.J. said, repeating what his uncle had told him back then. He'd almost forgotten about that day, it had been so long ago. After T.J.'s dad had left, Uncle Raymond had become like a dad to T.J., at least until T.J.'s mother had remarried. "He said if he ever wanted to be on the water, it would be on a sailboat." He looked at Rick. "I can't believe he told you that."

Rick's eyes were a soft, dark brown. Maybe that's why his uncle confided in him. Something in those eyes let you know this guy wasn't going to laugh at you for being silly or sentimental, or make fun of you for trying something you weren't good at. Perfect qualities for an instructor.

"He likes to talk when he's nervous," Rick said. "And he's pretty proud of you." He looked away. "He talked about you a lot. I was hoping I'd get the chance to meet you."

Okay, now that was a lot to take in all at once. T.J. never realized that his uncle got nervous about anything. Up until Aunt Gladdie left, Raymond had always seemed like a pillar of strength and certainty. As odd as it felt to know that, the thing that really struck T.J. was that Rick had wanted to meet him.

Hoped to meet him.

"Did he tell you I was gay?" T.J. asked.

Rick shrugged. "Not in so many words, but I picked up on it. I tend to keep my personal life to myself when I'm teaching, so no, I don't think your uncle was trying to talk you up for any particular reason. He's genuinely proud of you."

Wow. T.J. didn't know what to say.

They shared a basket of fried clams accompanied by a good local microbrew. Once the food showed up, the conversation flowed easily. T.J. learned that Rick had had a semi-serious relationship for three years before it imploded.

"He got jealous," Rick said. "I don't screw around, but my job puts me in contact with a lot of people. He couldn't handle that."

That had been in Southern California. After the relationship ended, Rick had moved north. He'd answered an ad for sailing instructor two summers ago. He'd never planned on staying, but he liked the area and the people.

"What do you do in the winter?" T.J. asked. "I mean, isn't this a seasonal occupation?"

Rick nodded. "It is. Nobody wants to learn how to sail in December." He shrugged. "Last winter I worked as a personal trainer. I don't have anything lined up yet, although the gym said they'd take me back." He scrunched up his nose. "The women hit on me, though. The minute they start to get in shape—" He made a WTF gesture with his hands. "I don't get it. I'm not the most effeminate gay man in the world, but it's not like I come on to them."

T.J. chuckled, thinking about the woman on the rescue boat. "Happens to me, too, but probably not as often."

Rick gave him the once-over again. "Oh, I don't know about that. Put you in a gym in bicycle shorts and a tank top, and every woman—and half the men—would be after you."

T.J. felt a flush creep into his cheeks. "I don't think so."

"Are you nuts? Not only are you a good-looking guy, you're a nice guy. You bought your lonely uncle sailing lessons because of something he said to you as a kid. You're a total chick magnet."

Rick had just given him an opening. T.J. took a deep breath and crossed mental fingers. He tried to give Rick a sexy, corner of the eye glance. "How about a guy magnet?"

He felt stupid as soon as he said it, but it was too late to take it back.

Luckily for him, Rick smiled. "A total guy magnet."

After that, they moved from the bar to the restaurant proper. Before T.J. knew it, a couple of hours had passed in pleasant conversation tinged every now and then with a flirtatious remark. A nice little nervous anticipation was building in his belly, but he still didn't have a clue where this was going. It didn't have the feel of a random hookup, but then again, no matter what Rick said, T.J. didn't believe a guy like Rick—sexy, easygoing, athletic Rick—would want anything other than a random hookup with someone like him.

They split the bill for dinner. When T.J. took out his cell to call a cab, Rick stopped him. "How about I give you a ride home? Or to your uncle's, if you think that's where he took your car."

"You don't have to do that." Not that T.J. wouldn't mind being in a car with Rick, but the man had already spent hours with him.

They were standing on the boardwalk outside the restaurant. The lake looked silver in the moonlight. Soft yellow streetlights illuminated the footpath around the lake. A few nighttime dog walkers were out, but other than that, the area was deserted.

Rick moved in close. "I know I don't have to," he said, his voice low. "I want to."

He'd stopped just shy of touching T.J. *Up to me*, T.J. thought. Rick was leaving the rest up to him.

What the hell. He could survive a random hookup, couldn't he? Even if it was with a guy he wouldn't mind seeing for more than just one night?

He closed the distance and kissed Rick lightly on the lips. He felt Rick grin against his mouth, and then Rick took over the kiss.

When they broke apart a few moments later, T.J. was out of breath and his cock was pressing pretty insistently against the zipper of his jeans. Rick was one hell of a kisser.

"Uh, yeah," T.J. managed to say. "Sure. I could use a ride home." Fuck the car. He could deal with that tomorrow.

They kissed again when they got inside Rick's car. This time they were both breathing hard when the kiss ended. Rick took T.J.'s hand and put it on the considerable bulge beneath his linen pants. T.J. squeezed, and Rick groaned.

"How far away do you live?" Rick asked.

"A couple of miles."

"Oh, good. I think I can make that."

T.J. squeezed again.

"Well, not if you keep that up," Rick said. His eyes were deep and dark, his mouth hungry as he pulled T.J. in for another kiss.

T.J.'s own cock was demanding attention, but he wanted more than a hand job in the front seat of a car. He let go and pulled away from the kiss. "Then I guess we'd better go."

They managed to make it up the stairs to T.J.'s second-floor apartment before Rick grabbed him again. The man loved to kiss, not that T.J. minded. Especially not when Rick pressed him up against the inside of his front door and shoved his hand down the inside of T.J.'s jeans.

The feel of Rick's hand on him was amazing. All the lust that had been building up throughout dinner took over, and T.J.'s brain short-circuited. He propelled Rick down the short hallway to the bedroom, shedding his shirt along the way and then going to work on Rick's linen pants. By the time they reached the bed, Rick was naked from the waist down and T.J. from the waist up. It didn't take long for them to get rid of the rest of their clothes, and then Rick was on him.

The guy was definitely a top. T.J. didn't mind that, either, not with the kind of things that Rick could do with his mouth, and not just to T.J.'s cock. Rick used his tongue and lips on parts of T.J.'s body that he'd never known were erogenous zones. By the time they got around to actually fucking, T.J.'s skin was so sensitized, he thought he might come just from a breath of air across his nipples.

As it was, it didn't take T.J. long. Rick's cock was long and thick, and it felt wonderful pounding into him. He hadn't had a man in his bed in far too long, and he'd never had a man like Rick before. T.J. came fast and hard, and then went along for the ride as Rick worked to make himself come.

Afterward, T.J. sprawled on his back, enjoying the pleasant buzz. Rick stirred after a moment and sat up.

Was he leaving already? Maybe T.J. had misread the whole thing, and this was just Rick's version of a random hookup.

"I have a confession to make," Rick said.

His back was to T.J., so T.J. couldn't see his face. T.J. frowned. Confessions after sex were never a good thing, right?

"I set this up," Rick said softly.

"What?"

Rick looked at T.J. over his shoulder. "With your uncle. To take your car so you'd need a ride home."

Now T.J. sat up in bed. "I don't get it," he said.

"I wanted to meet you. Your uncle told me so much about you, how you haven't dated in a while, and—"

Okay, now T.J. got it, and he wasn't happy about it. "So you thought I'd be an easy lay. Well, congratulations, you got what you—"

"No, that's not it at all." Rick turned around, and T.J. got a good look at his eyes. The guy wasn't a player. He really cared what T.J. thought of him. "Your uncle said he'd bring you this afternoon, that you were a good swimmer and could be the guy overboard. He said it could be a way for me to meet you. When I pulled your uncle out of the water, he was tired, yeah, but the reason he wanted to go back to the dock was because I'd told him I liked you and I was thinking about asking you out, and he said he had a surefire way to make that happen."

"So that's why you guys left me stranded on the safety boat with Nancy with the wandering fingers." She'd sat next to him and actually started rubbing T.J.'s shoulders before he'd told her he batted for the other team. "So I'd be out of the way while my uncle lifted my car."

"I didn't know he was going to do that."

"But you played along with it after the fact."

Rick looked down at the bed. "Yeah," he said. "Yeah, I did. I'd say I'm sorry, but I'm really not." He glanced up at T.J. "Not with the way things turned out. At least, not so far, anyway."

A part of T.J. was still annoyed that his uncle and Rick had played him, but it was a very small part. A bigger part wondered what happened now.

"So," he said, turning to face Rick. "Now that we've gotten the confession out of the way, where do you see this going?"

"You're not angry?"

T.J. shrugged. "No one's ever gone to so much trouble to meet me before, and at least now I know my uncle hasn't turned to a life of crime." It also explained why his uncle hadn't answered his cell. "Although I'm not sure I like the fact that he thinks he can play matchmaker for me."

"You don't?"

"I didn't mean this time," T.J. said quickly. "I enjoyed this one a lot." He grinned. "A hell of a lot."

Rick got up on his hands and knees and stalked over to T.J. "Oh, yeah? Feel like enjoying it some more?"

T.J.'s cock twitched. Apparently that part of his anatomy liked the idea. He snaked an arm around the back of Rick's neck and pulled him down until they were both lying on the bed.

"I take it that's a yes," Rick said.

T.J. kissed him. "That's a yes." A most definite yes.

If things went the way T.J. hoped they would, his uncle would be out of the matchmaking business, maybe for good.

"Just one thing," T.J. said when they finished the kiss.

"Hmm?"

"Did my uncle pass his lesson?" T.J. hated to think that his uncle had screwed up his last lesson on purpose and wouldn't be able to sail on his own if he wanted to.

"Well, we might have to redo that last one," Rick said. "But I won't charge him for it."

"You won't?"

Rick grinned. "If you agree to play man overboard again."

T.J. pulled Rick back down for another kiss. "Anytime," he said. "Anytime."

CRUISING

Dominic Santi

I get seasick in a fucking rowboat. I spend my days downtown in a suit or hiking in the mountains. I hate the water. But my partner Brendan is an assistant recreation director on a major cruise ship. He spends damn near half his life on the ocean. He has sun-bleached blond hair and sparkling blue eyes and his toned, slender body has a deep sailor's tan with no tan lines. From the moment I met him at an AIDS Project LA fundraiser, I knew he was The One for me. We were both in our early thirties, and we loved the same types of theater and dancing and we were both gourmet cooks. We fucked like weasels every day he was in port.

I was so crazy about him I convinced myself that the "one minor difference" between us didn't matter—enough so that I hadn't yet gotten around to mentioning it to him, even after two years together and our becoming domestic partners last spring. Every time he found me a "great deal" for a vacation trip on his ship, I somehow managed to have to work, or to help my uncle or a friend move, or the dog needed dental work that couldn't be put off.

"Next time, babe," I'd say, laughing, and he'd grin and we'd end up fucking on the floor of whatever room we were in.

Two months ago, he came home from his latest twenty-day "voyage" damn near dancing on air. The cruise line had finally gotten on board with he called "the whole family equality thing." Same-sex spouses and domestic partners were now eligible for the incredibly discounted rates offered on select cruises to families of employees. As soon as the word came down, Brendan had picked the perfect cruise for the first anniversary of our commitment ceremony: fifteen "glorious days" sailing from Los Angeles to Fort Lauderdale by way of one of Brendan's favorite places in the whole world—the Panama Canal.

"Sweetie, this is going to be perfect!" he crowed, hauling me into his arms and peppering me with his drugging kisses. "We're talking Mexico, Nicaragua, Aruba—and the Canal! I am so going to fuck you senseless in the ports of your dreams!"

All I could think of as he hauled me off to fuck me senseless in our own comfortable bedroom was *this is so fucking not going to be great!*

In the interim between that night and that day of our embarkation, the time had still never quite been right to bring up the little problem I had being on the water. The closer the date got, the more I suddenly found reasons to work late on the days he was home—and when I did get home from work, to go directly to bed, "sorry, babe, I'm exhausted!" while he was still up. If all else failed and I couldn't avoid him, as soon as he brought up the subject, I distracted him with a blow job that left him so wasted he forgot about everything else.

I pretended I didn't notice how he was getting a little bit distant, too. Fuck, Brendan's so fucking gorgeous! And he's

smart and funny and responsible and pretty much everything I'd
ever wanted in a partner. I was so horny with missing him, I was
jerking off every day in the shower, which with the schedule I'd
set for myself didn't leave nearly enough time for sex with him.
More than once, he'd asked me if there was anything we needed
to talk about. The day before we left, he pointedly demanded
to know "right now, dammit!" if there was anything he needed
to know.

There sure as hell wasn't. I just laughed and kissed him and
ignored his frustrated look, telling him once again that I was just
working extra to keep on track with our plan to make double
payments on the condo mortgage so we wouldn't have to worry
about money on the trip or later on. When he'd finally packed
both our bags and was waiting impatiently at the van taking us
to the port, I plastered a big fake grin on my face and jogged out
the door, quite a bit later than he was comfortable leaving for
a cruise. During our rush through LA's early-afternoon traffic,
all I could do was hope for a traffic jam or for the ship to have
mechanical trouble or even for a fucking earthquake—anything
so the whole mess would blow over and I suddenly wouldn't
have to go anywhere near Brendan's fucking ocean, much less
get on board his fucking ship. Which, of course, sure as hell
wasn't the way things worked out.

"You get seasick?!" The not-entirely-unexpected incredulity in
his voice did nothing to quiet my stomach. "Christ, I thought
you wanted a divorce!"

Now, that was enough to drag me out of my misery. I carefully lifted the cold cloth he'd laid across my forehead and looked
tentatively up at him. Just the motion of my eyeballs moving had
my stomach rebelling again, though there was no doubt it was
already completely empty. I groaned and closed my eyes.

"Open your eyes, dammit!"

"I can't. I'll puke." Again. I lay as still as I could on the bunk while Brendan put another cold cloth on my neck. I didn't think I'd ever been more miserable in my life.

"Keeping your eyes open helps. And you're not going to be sick any more, at least not now. The Compazine should be kicking in. It *always* works."

My face heated just thinking about how and where the drug was dissolving into my bloodstream—the drug prescribed and administered by Brendan's friend and occasional fuck buddy, the ship's doctor, who'd made a cabin call as a special favor because Brendan had been so upset at how ill I was. If there was a more embarrassing way to be spending my anniversary, I couldn't think of it. Then I remembered the rest of Brendan's words.

"A divorce?" I said, damn near sitting up on the bed. I moaned as I fell right back down. "Why the hell would I want a divorce? I love you!"

The movement had me so nauseous I was once again prostrate on the sweaty sheets. I groaned as Brendan washed my face with a cool cloth and laid a fresh cold pack on my neck. Just the sunlight coming in the window over the bed made my eyes hurt. The cold pack was heavenly.

"You didn't seem to want me around," he said quietly. "Every time I tried to talk to you about the trip—or anything!—you cut me off and had, you know, something more important to do. I thought maybe you were getting tired of me." He shrugged self-consciously. "I wondered if maybe you'd started seeing someone else while I was gone."

At my raised eyebrows, he blushed and looked away. "I started thinking I was being really stupid, working extra cruises for the mortgage and all, and so I could take time off for this trip. Maybe I'd been neglecting you so much you were taking up with somebody else instead."

How anybody so perfect could occasionally be so insecure always shocked me. But Brendan was damn near in tears. I took a deep breath and looked miserably up at him.

"No way is this your fucking fault. I didn't want to tell you I get seasick."

Both his eyebrows went up. He dropped the cloth on the nightstand.

"This is better?" There was an edge coming into his voice. Okay, pissed was better than dejected. I took a deep breath and tried to focus on him. Fuck. I hurt everywhere.

"No," I said miserably. "God, babe. I'm so sorry. I know how much you love being on the ocean, and I just suck at it. I kept hoping there'd be, I don't know, a typhoon or the cruise would be overbooked or my reservation would be miraculously canceled. Pretty much anything so I wouldn't have to tell you I get sick in a rowboat. Then we could keep going on like we were, with you going to work and having fun on your cruises and me going rock climbing and shit like that, then coming home and telling each other about what we'd done. And we could fuck and go dancing and cook together and do all the other fun stuff we do, and I wouldn't have to go anywhere near the fucking water."

"Or go on cruises with me," he sighed. "You asshole." He stood up and took his cell phone out of his pocket. "The first thing we need to do is get a different room, one with fresh air and more in the middle of the ship and lower down. That way you won't feel the rise and fall of the ocean so much."

The words "rise and fall" made me break out in another cold sweat. But I really was feeling better. Or at least I seemed to be done puking. I watched his crisp new khaki shorts hug his ass

as he strode around the tiny room, making arrangements for a
different room "amidships," whatever the hell that meant. Then
he pulled out his wallet and took out a credit card.

"Yeah, I know it's one hell of an upgrade. Just get us there
fast, okay? He's finally quit puking, but I don't know how much
longer he'll be awake now that the Compazine has kicked in."

Shit, the drugs were going to put me to sleep? Even as
I thought it, I yawned. Fuck, I was suddenly so tired I could
barely keep my eyes open.

"Not yet!" Brendan said, suddenly squatting next to me. He
slid his arm under my shoulders, the phone cricked in his ear.
"Thanks, man. I owe you one." He flipped the phone closed and
eased me to my feet. "Come on, hot stuff. We're relocating to
a honeymoon suite. That should be a whole lot easier on your
dainty equilibrium. But you have to get there under your own
power."

Twenty minutes later, I was ensconced naked on fresh, cool
white sheets in a suite the size of a premier hotel room. My
eyelids were so heavy I knew I was losing the battle to stay
awake. But the ocean seemed to have calmed. At least the room
wasn't swaying as much as it had been before. A cool breeze blew
in from the open door to the balcony. Brendan was seated in a
chair across from me, playing with his e-book reader. Damn,
he was so fucking gorgeous. And I was so in love with him. I
couldn't believe how much of an asshole I'd been.

"I'm so sorry, babe," I said, stifling another gigantic yawn.
The whole room was getting fuzzy. Then it was black.

I vaguely remembered getting up to use what Brendan called
"the head" during the night. He'd steered me back to bed and
spooned up in back of me, his dick poking me in the kidney as I
drifted back to sleep. The next thing I knew, sunlight streamed
in through the curtains billowing in front of the partly opened

balcony door. I carefully rolled over. I was queasy, but it wasn't too bad. On the nightstand, a note was propped next to a bottle of water, a couple packets of crackers, and my next dose of Compazine.

Compazine first. When your stomach is settled, nibble the crackers and take small sips of the water. I'll be back in a couple hours. I have to cover for a friend. Love you—you asshole.

I smiled, just a little bit, and followed orders. When I woke up again, Brendan was sitting naked in the chair by the bed again, jerking off.

"Don't move," he said, breathing hard as his hand moved slick and leisurely over his long, slender dick. It was deep red, a pearl of precum leaking from the beautiful cut head as he squeezed. His other hand tugged on his balls. They were dark red and climbing his shaft. Fuck, he was close! His nipples poked up hard from the mat of blond hair on his deeply tanned chest. His thighs flexed as he lifted his hips, stroking faster.

"I get so horny on the ocean," he panted. "I wanted to jerk off together with you, this first time. But I can't wait. I'm so fucking h-hard."

Despite the drugs fogging my system, I had a morning woody, too. I carefully eased the covers back with one foot and took my dick in my hand.

"Fuck," he whispered, his hand flying over his shaft.

I stroked up once, running my thumb over the already slick head. I looked him in the eye and licked my lips.

His eyes glazed and cum spurted up onto his chest. Fuck, I love the sounds Brendan makes when he's coming. He grunts and pants and fucks his dick up into his fist. Watching him come always makes me shoot. I shook, my eyes still locked on his as the most awesome fucking orgasm I'd felt in a long time rocked my entire body.

"I love you," I whispered.

"I love you, too," he panted, tipping his head back and closing his eyes, shuddering as he squeezed the last drops from his shaft. "And you're still an asshole."

I stroked my thoroughly spent cock, watching his breathing slow. When he opened his eyes again, he smiled and stood up, holding his hand out to me. "Let's go take a shower. Then we're going to have a light breakfast on the balcony and walk around the ship. The fresh air and moving will help acclimate you."

I let him pull me gingerly to my feet. My stomach still wasn't happy, but it was better than it had been the night before.

"Don't worry," Brendan said, squeezing my hand. "The Compazine should hold you for a while, and I've got some Sea-Bands for you. We'll stop by Jeff's office and see what other meds will work for you. Maybe you'll feel well enough by tonight to fuck me."

Jeff. The ship's doctor. My face heated, but as I opened my mouth to speak, Brendan smiled and squeezed my ass.

"Or maybe I'll just fuck you."

That would work, too! I grinned back at him like an idiot. In the daylight, I could see the clear-walled shower was big enough for two. Brendan loved fucking in the shower. All I had to do was keep my stomach settled.

That turned out to be easier said than done. I slavishly followed Jeff's directions, but I missed most of the first port call in Mexico. I was zonked out on meds that, thank god, I was finally able to swallow. Brendan was disappointed. He'd wanted to give me an anniversary blow job on a special lovers' beach. But when I woke up enough to go down to the pier and walk on the beach, the sight of Brendan's ass moving beneath his bright holiday board shorts had my dick swelling, which had the anticipated reciprocal hard-on-inducing effect on my apparently perpetually-horny-on-the-water lover.

The Sea-Bands helped as we got under way again. I still wasn't up for dinner in any of the ship's fancy restaurants, so Brendan ordered a surprisingly delicious chicken soup and breadsticks for dinner.

"It helps to know the cook." He'd grinned, wiggling his fingers at me in a way that let me know exactly how well he knew the cook.

Then he took me out on the balcony to watch the moon on the water. The breeze was cool, so he brought a light cotton blanket from the closet to throw over us as we sat in our lounge chairs. The smell of the salt water was so much cleaner than it was on the beach, the sound of the waves and the quiet vibration of the ship's engines totally relaxing. The room lights glowed behind us, the white floor-to-ceiling balcony dividers separating us from everyone else on the ship. In front of us, there was nothing but clear, waist-high glass panels between us and the water. It was like we were alone on the ocean.

Brendan turned out the lights behind us. Something plunked onto the white metal table beside me. Brendan knelt beside me and tunneled under the blanket. He unzipped my shorts. Then his breath was hot on my crotch as he pulled my dick free.

"Mmm. I love the taste of your cock."

I gasped as he swallowed me, drawing me deep into his throat as my dick reached for his tonsils. He came up for air and I grabbed his head.

"What if somebody sees us!"

His fist stayed tight on my dick, jerking me off with his spit. He laughed and the tip of his tongue swiped my balls.

"Who the hell is going to see us? China is a long way off!"

He was right. There was nothing and no one in front of us. The only things in my world were the ocean and Brendan, who was once more busily sucking my cock. I bucked as he tickled his tongue into my piss slit.

"Fuck, I love how you give head!"

He laughed and tugged on my balls, working his tongue over my shaft and the hypersensitive V below the crown.

"I'd be even more enthusiastic," he mumbled around my dick, "if you stuffed some of that lube on the table up my ass and fingered me while I jerk off. I am so fucking horny!"

I was not going to turn down an offer like that. I jerked his shorts down to his knees. His gorgeous naked butt cheeks stuck out from under the blanket, glowing in the moonlight. I grabbed the lube from the table and slathered it over my hand. I stoked down his crack, groaning as my fingers found the heat of his sphincter. It quivered against me, kissing my fingertip in as I pressed. One finger, two, three. Fuck, he was ready!

My other hand was still under the blanket, resting lightly on his hair. "Suck me!" I growled, and shoved his head down.

He took me all the way down his throat. He was still tugging my balls, but I could hear the slap, slap, slap of his other hand working his dick now. The drugs slowed my reactions. He came twice before I did, licking and sucking and swallowing my dick as he ground his ass into my hand. His asscheeks bucked against me in the moonlight, his asshole squeezing my glistening fingers like I was a living dildo. Each time he came, his throat worked my dick until eventually I saw stars, too.

By the next port of call, I'd adjusted enough to go on excursions with him. I'd never dreamed jungles could be so beautiful, or beaches so warm and pristine.

"Why do you ever come home?" I'd asked him, awestruck as a flock of parrots zoomed over our gondola above the rainforest.

"Because you're there." He'd smiled, love shining in his eyes as he bumped his knee into me. He was hard again. He was always hard when the ocean was near. And his addiction was starting to wear off on me.

I had to wear Sea-Bands most of the time we were at sea, and Jeff came up with a cocktail that kept me awake and my stomach mostly settled. Brendan taught me how to walk down the ship's passageways and outside on the decks with the least upheaval to my equilibrium. I made it through the Panama Canal—which truly was one of the most astounding things I'd ever seen—and to the second formal dinner, where I did Brendan proud in my tuxedo when he introduced me to his captain.

From the look the captain gave me, I was pretty sure not much on the man's ship escaped him, including my asinine behavior. I managed to hide my blush from Brendan, telling tasteful, witty stories and eventually leading a line dance that was one of the hits of the evening. When we finally retired, the captain nodded his approval to Brendan. As the last bit of tension left my lover's shoulders, I realized how much it truly meant to him to have me on the cruise. I took him back to our room and this time I initiated the fucking, much to our mutual pleasure.

Eventually I was able to start hanging out in the on-board pools and Jacuzzis, and I got into the movies under the stars, the shows, and the massage cabanas. Hell, Brendan even taught me to play shuffleboard.

The last night at sea, we were once again on the balcony in the dark. This time, we were naked and he was the one lying on the lounge chair. I was on top of him, my back to his chest, my legs straddling his as my ass muscles milked the incredible shaft impaling me. He wouldn't let me touch myself, so my hands gripped the top of the chair on either side of his head, helping me balance as I raised and lowered my hips, fucking my ass over his cock. One of his hands was wrapped around my dick, the other was pulling my balls. My nipples were stiff from the sea breeze blowing over us. Our skin was barely visible in a moonless sky as the quiet sound of the waves rushed past us.

"I'm so horny!" I panted, shuddering at the feel of his cock sliding through my asshole, of his hand stroking my dick. "I'm going to come so fucking hard!"

"I know, sweetie," he whispered, sucking the back of my neck. "You set the pace. As fast or as slow as you want. I'm not going to come until you do."

I arched above him. "Gonna come!" Oh, god! My balls were climbing my dick. Brendan was tugging on them, rolling them in his fingers as he jerked my cock. His shaft was hitting my prostate with each thrust, pressing the cum from me. I tightened my legs, pounding my ass onto him, clenching him, loving him.

"Whenever you want, sweetie," he purred. "This one is all for you."

"For you," I gasped.

He tightened his grip and squeezed, his cock hitting my joy spot at just the perfect angle. I arched up, yelling, his hips following mine as hot fountains of cum spurted through my dick. They rained down onto my chest and abs, covering his still-stroking hand as his dick stretched my hole wider, wider. He jerked beneath me, his yell echoing in my ear as he came up my ass. I shook until my legs gave out, then fell back hard onto him.

Brendan was laughing, and fuck, that was a sound I so purely loved to hear. I stood up enough for him to throw the rubber onto the table. I'd been so loud, I'd been afraid somebody would have heard us and complained. But the sound was lost in the ocean, along with the rest of my fears. Damn, I'd been such an asshole. We lay there talking about the cruise and all the things we'd done until his legs started going to sleep.

When we finally went inside and climbed into the shower, I asked him when would be a good time for us to take our next cruise. He laughed for so long I thought he was going to choke. Tears were running down his face when he finally caught his breath enough to say he'd show me the links when we got home. For now, he was too damn tired to even think about it. So we crawled into bed and slept.

There's a cruise to Alaska next summer. We're going to go on that together, then maybe do an Aegean voyage with one of his sister ships. I have prescriptions and Sea-Bands on hand so I'll be ready whenever the next family cruise opportunity comes up, too. In the meanwhile, I'm working double shifts, saving up for our next vacation. But I'm only doing it while he's at sea now. And we're only doing double payments on the condo four times a year. Our time together is just too important to fuck around with, unless we're actually getting to fuck.

I'm one asshole who's learned his lesson.

RIVER GUIDE

Lou Harper

B rian liked his summer job. To some people, standing on the deck of a small boat giving the same hour-long spiel along the same route on the river, day after day, would be dull. Brian didn't think so. Sure, he knew his speech by heart, but that only made things easier. He still loved the ride from the Navy Pier up on the Chicago River, and he still loved the unique view it gave of the city.

The truth is, no two trips were the same. The time of day, the angle of the sun hitting the skyscrapers, and the weather made every trip different. Most of all it was the passengers. Putting nineteen strangers on a boat was like a chemical experiment. Even though all they were supposed to do was sit and listen, just by the virtue of being there and mixed together they created a distinct atmosphere. Brian liked observing people. Thanks to his practice, all he had to do was take a quick glance ashore to make sure none of the buildings had absconded overnight. Other than that he had plenty of opportunity to study the passengers.

Every once in a while he would even have the chance to get to know one a little more intimately. Yeah, being a tour guide was a great gig.

People taking the Chicago Architectural River Tour came from all over the world. It was funny how often they fit the stereotypes. And then there were those who just didn't seem to fit. Like that man on Brian's 11:30 tour—he was like an island in a sea of people. A very enticing, elegant island. Brian estimated the man's age as early- to mid-forties. He had a trim figure and handsome face of beautifully chiseled features—the kind of man who would only get more scrumptious with age. The wrinkles settling at the corner of his eyes indicated that he liked to laugh. That cloak of melancholy he wore was a poor fit on him, yet there it was.

When the boat reached the turning-around point, they took a short break, giving the passengers a chance to visit the bar. Melancholy Man stood by the railing, staring into the water like there was something deeply meaningful in its polluted depths. Brian chose the moment to make his move. He walked over and leaned on the rail next to the man, elbow to elbow. They were about the same height, but the other man had a much slimmer build than Brian.

"The river gets dyed bright green for St. Patrick's Day every year, but it has a pronounced green tint year-round because of the algae," Brian said, in way of breaking the ice.

The other man looked up with momentary confusion, but then arranged his expression into the semblance of a polite smile. "I didn't know that."

"You should see it; it's the same color as the slime in *Ghostbusters*. I mean, when it's dyed, not the algae. By the way, my name is Brian, Brian Ribeiro. It's Portuguese for 'little river.'" Brian offered his hand along with the self-introduction.

"Carl Erickson. It's nice to meet you," the man replied, taking Brian's hand. His smile was a genuine one this time. He had sensuous lips, fit for kissing, Brian noticed.

"Erickson. What kind of name is that, Swedish?"

"Norwegian. There are a bunch of us up there in Wisconsin."

So he was a tourist. Brian guessed as much. Good, he liked brief affairs with no entanglements.

"What is it like there?" he asked, to keep the conversation going. He knew he was sending out subtle signals of invitation with his whole body, even his voice.

"Do you ever listen to Garrison Keillor on NPR?" Carl was more relaxed now, but seemingly oblivious to Brian's signals.

"Sometimes. *Prairie Home Companion?*"

He quoted the quirky radio show's tag line: "Yes. It's just like Lake Wobegon. 'Where all the women are strong, all the men are good-looking, and all the children are above average.'"

"Wait, I thought that was Minnesota."

"Same difference."

There were faint sparkles of mischief dancing in Carl's eyes now, a sight that made Brian's cock jump up like an eager puppy.

He would have liked to fully peel Carl out of that coat of woe, maybe run his fingers through the neatly trimmed salt-and-pepper hair, but the break was over and he had to go.

"Well, it's certainly true about the men," Brian said, and winked at Carl before returning to his post.

For the next half an hour Brian felt Carl's gaze raking over his body, near constantly. He was glad that the loose cargo pants hid his excitement. He liked this part of the mating ritual, the prolonged foreplay: he enjoyed being wanted. Hell, if he wasn't afraid his parents would find out he probably would've done well as a male go-go dancer. It wasn't likely he'd meet anyone as classy as Carl, though.

Brian expected Carl to fall behind so they could exchange a few necessary words, arrange a time to meet later. To his dismay, Carl returned to land amidst the other passengers, without giving Brian a single backwards glance. Bitter disappointment and sexual frustration chewed Brian's guts. *You win some, you lose some,* he told himself, but it failed to make him feel any better.

Brian conducted his next tour as professionally as ever, but without much enthusiasm. He was glad it was his last one for the day and was relieved to hand the boat over to Joan, the second-shift guide.

Another enjoyable thing about the job was that it left him with plenty of free time. Time he suddenly didn't know what to do with. He decided to pop into the Art Institute before heading home. He figured the Cartier-Bresson special exhibit would provide a couple of hours of diversion. He'd seen the exhibit twice before, but he kept finding new interesting details in the old photographs.

Some of the grainy black-and-white prints were getting close to a century in age, yet the people in them were so very much alive. They weren't stiff and posed; the photographer's camera caught them in moments both mundane and real. Time kept flowing around them, through them, even as they stood frozen, fixed in silver. Looking at those photos was similar to reading only one intriguing sentence from a book and wondering about the rest. Like Carl, the enigma, they captured Brian's imagination.

One of Brian's weaknesses was his impatience. He'd given up on mystery novels because he always ended up skipping to the end to find out who the killer was. The mystery of Carl bugged him more than anything in a long time. Carl was a story Brian knew nothing about, not even the beginning, not to mention the end. Aside from the curiosity, he found the man fucking hot. Brian wasn't normally into older men—they reminded him of his father too much—but Carl was something completely different. And completely unreachable.

It kept bugging him as he took the El to his apartment in Lakeview, while he fixed himself dinner, and even as he tried to zonk out in front of the television. He had a quick wank but it was a hollow satisfaction. Finally Brian realized he needed a stronger distraction. So he took a shower, spruced himself up and went out.

It was a weeknight, but it was also Boystown, so there was always something going on. The bars were busy enough, and men gave him interested looks, but Brian couldn't see anyone he liked. Buck's was the third place he popped into. He went straight to the bar and asked for a beer. Brian sort of knew Joe, the bartender, so they got to chatting while Brian scanned the room for potential hookups. What he spotted at the other end of the bar made him stop in mid-sentence.

"What? You look like you saw a ghost," Joe asked.

"Seren-fucking-dipity, Joe," Brian replied, not taking his eyes off the man with the salt-and-pepper hair.

He grabbed his beer and briskly walked up to Carl. The seats on both sides of this Man of Mystery were taken, so Brian wedged himself in the empty space between stools, moving closer to Carl than was strictly necessary.

"Hi there. Funny meeting you here," Brian said to break the ice yet again.

He witnessed the same show as last time; Carl turned toward him with the air of a man rising from deep water. His face arranged itself into a mask of joviality, with a touch of confusion.

"Sorry, have we met?" he asked with a slight slur.

"Yeah, this morning on the boat. Remember?"

A crack appeared in Carl's mask. "River Spirit! You've left your post."

It made Brian smile. "Don't worry, there are other spirits to take over."

"At this hour?"

"Well, there are river taxis, at least. You should try that sometime. It's really beautiful."

"I know," he said with a pensive smile.

"So you've been?"

"Long time ago. Will loved it." Carl drew his brows together, as if he was surprised or even displeased at what he'd just said. He turned his focus back on Brian. "Brian, right? And your last name means river in...Spanish?"

"Portuguese."

"I'm very sorry. I'm afraid I'm a touch inebriated."

"Not a problem."

Spotting an open booth, Brian tugged at Carl's shirt. "Come, let's sit over there. It's more comfortable."

As soon as they sat down, Carl was getting up again. "Let me get you a drink."

Brian had no intention of letting Carl go anywhere. Who knew, he might bolt for the door. Brian knew second chances like this didn't come by often, and he was going to hang on to it. So he quickly stood up and pushed Carl back into his seat. "I'll get it. What will you have?"

"Old-fashioned."

A minute later, back with their drinks, Brian found Carl gazing wistfully at the people around them. His body filled the booth with the liquid languidness that alcohol brings, but his eyes gleamed sharp and lucid. As they tracked his every movement, Brian began to feel that prickling thrill of being wanted. Oh yeah, Carl was on the hook, but he was skittish for some reason, and Brian had to careful reeling him in.

"So what do you do up there in dairy land?" he asked to keep up the pretense of polite conversation.

Carl took a sip of his cocktail. "I'm a veterinarian."

"Puppies and kittens?"

"Livestock. Mostly cows, the occasional horse or pig. The town I live in has a population of three hundred thousand and twice as many dairy cows. At least it seems like it."

"I would've never figured you for a vet," Brian admitted.

"What, then?"

"Retired male fashion model."

Carl chortled into his glass. "You're saying I'm old."

Brian stretched his legs out under the table, taking Carl's lower limbs captive. "Like a bottle of twenty-five-year-old whiskey is old."

Fumes of pheromones and alcohol hung heavily between them. Brian leaned forward and took one of Carl's hands into his own. He unfurled it, gently touching the palm and long fingers. Carl's fingers seemed too delicate for a country vet, but the calluses on them belied their appearance.

Brian didn't miss the quickening of Carl's breath, the rush of blood heating up his cheeks. It matched his own state of arousal.

Yet Carl pulled his hand away. "Brian, Brian, Brian. What does a nubile young thing want from an old goat like me?"

Brian shrugged. "What does anyone want? You're a very sexy old goat, you know."

"I like your directness."

"I thought earlier, on the boat, that you were undressing me with your eyes. Was I wrong?"

"You weren't. I was undressing you. Anything less would've been an insult to your beauty." There was playfulness in his tone, but he was still holding himself at a frustrating arm's length away.

It only made Brian want to push harder. He leaned forward more, into Carl's personal space. Under the table his legs held Carl's tightly.

"You're a randy old goat, then—a very fuckable randy old goat. I bet you're kinky too," Brian murmured suggestively.

Carl's breath hitched, and for the first time Brian saw the naked, unadulterated lust rise to the surface in Carl's eyes. "Come back to my hotel," Carl whispered, almost shy.

Brian felt the smug excitement of a cat who'd just gotten to the well hidden cream. "Let's go. Where are you staying?"

"The Majestic."

"Fancy," he said approvingly, and put his arm around Carl's waist as they left the bar.

They took a cab although the hotel wasn't far away. Brian wanted to keep Carl in a confined space till they got back to the hotel, not giving the night air a chance to blow away the sexual tension between them. They both acted with reasonable decorum till they stepped inside the suite. After that all bets were off. Carl held Brian's head with his hands and kissed him with an unexpected hunger. Brian occupied his own hands massaging Carl's small, tight ass. Their hard cocks rubbed together through too many layers of denim and cotton. Brian went for the belt on Carl's pants.

Carl stopped him. "Wait. I'd like you to do something for me."

Brian pulled back a little to look Carl in the eye. "Something kinky?"

"A little. I'd like to watch you undress."

"Like a strip show?"

"No, nothing so tacky, but go slow."

Carl extricated himself from Brian's arms and sat down at the edge of the bed. He looked up expectantly. Brian didn't mind being watched, generally enjoyed it, and the desire darkening Carl's eyes was a definite turn-on. Fortunately, he had on a button-down shirt that night. He undid the buttons one by one from top to bottom. The whole time he watched Carl, and didn't miss how the man pressed his hand on the bulge of his pants. Brian pushed the shirt over his shoulders and let it slip to the floor. He ran one hand down his chest to his cock and kneaded it for a few seconds.

The leather belt slid out of its loops and landed next to the shirt. Brian undid the button on his fly and pulled the zipper down in a painfully slow motion. He pushed his jeans down, but only a few inches. Brian's cock, free from its confinement, sprang up and poked its flared purple head out of his briefs. Carl's lips parted and his tongue flicked out. Brian knew what Carl wanted and would be happy to give it to him, but not before turning up the heat some more. With his thumb he spread the precum around his cockhead. Carl's groan let Brian know he was on target. Brian pushed his jeans and briefs the rest of the way down and stepped out of them. He also took a couple of steps forward so his cock swung only a few inches from Carl's lips.

"It's yours. Come and get it," Brian said, giving his cock a few lazy strokes.

Carl's knees hit the carpet with a dull thud. He put his lips on Brian's cockhead, almost with reverence. He glided his tongue around the ridge, teasing the spot on the underside. When Carl licked down Brian's shaft, Brian widened his stance to let Carl suck his balls into that warm mouth, one by one.

"Stroke yourself," Brian instructed him.

Carl dutifully took his cock out and begun to slide his hand over it. His other hand kept massaging Brian's sac. The wet heat of Carl's mouth soon enveloped Brian's cockhead again. Brian reached down to pet that fine jaw, to dig his fingers into the wiry hair.

"Fuck, so good," he groaned.

Carl looked up, eyes filled with gratitude. He redoubled his efforts and soon he swallowed most of Brian's cock down. An impressive feat, since Brian was a big boy. Brian lost himself to the assault, lost control somewhere, only vaguely aware that he was roughly grasping Carl's head, thrusting his hips forward. Even worse, he didn't care. Carl's hands on his ass, holding him tight, convinced Brian it was okay. The last vestige of Brian's self-control asserted itself as his balls drew up. He tugged at Carl's hair, but Carl just held on tighter. So Brian let go, feeling Carl's throat constrict as he swallowed Brian's jizz. At last when Brian's trembling legs couldn't possibly support him any longer, Carl let him go. Brian plopped on the edge of the bed. He realized with shame he had no idea if Carl came or not. He was about to ask, but then the sight of a glob of cum on his foot answered the question. He wiped it off with the corner of the bed linen.

"Damn, Carl, that was one fine blow job. If anyone ever calls you a cocksucker, be proud."

"Who said I wasn't?"

"Was I too rough? I think I lost it there at one point."

"You were perfect," Carl said, standing up. "You guessed right that I had kinks, but then who doesn't?"

Brian pulled Carl to him. "Let's get you out of these clothes already. You make me feel self-conscious."

"So you're staying the night?"

"Of course I am. The night's young, and we've barely gotten started."

Brian was still extremely intrigued with Carl's pert ass and hoped Carl would let him fuck him. However, Brian's dick needed a moment or two to recover. He figured he could use the time to untangle the mystery of Carl. Once they were both naked and under the covers he rolled to his side, facing Carl. He propped his head on his elbow and lay his upper leg over Carl's legs.

"What happened to Will?" he asked.

"What?" Carl looked at him with alarm.

"Will—you mentioned him earlier. He means something, doesn't he? What happened to him?"

Carl gave a sigh of surrender. "He left me after fifteen years together. We used to go on a vacation together every summer. All over the world, Paris, Rio De Janeiro, you name it."

"And this year you came to exotic Chicago, all by yourself."

"I didn't have the motivation for anything more."

"If you don't mind me asking, why did he leave?"

"Midlife crisis."

"Huh?"

"He was...used to be a true bear, big and hairy. I loved that about him. But I guess he didn't love himself quite the same. Something happened to him when he turned forty-five. He started working out, dieting, dying his hair. He even got his body waxed. In a year he was a completely different man. Then he got himself a convertible and moved to San Francisco."

"That's harsh, man."

"I can't really blame him. It's his life. He's fulfilling some boyhood dream."

"And what about you?"

"What about me?"

"I'm guessing it's not easy to find somebody over in cow country."

A muscle in Carl's face twitched involuntarily, and he closed his eyes.

"Wait a minute. There's somebody, isn't there?"

"Mmm."

"I bet he's a brown-eyed kid following you everywhere like a puppy, and you're a total bastard to him."

Carl kept his eyes closed and his mouth shut.

"Look at me," Brian said in a firm voice.

Carl complied, obviously not able to resist a direct command. "Blond, blue-eyed, two-hundred-something pounds of pure muscle, but yeah, I've been a total bastard to him."

"Why? You don't like him?"

"I like him very much."

"Then what's the problem?"

Carl heaved a sigh. "He's too young, for one thing—"

Brian snorted. "Bullshit excuse."

"And there is the other thing. Will and I were cut of the same cloth. When your sexual preferences run to the exotic side, it's hard to bring that up to a potential date, especially if you're fifteen years out of dating practice."

Brian broke out in a hearty laugh. "You kinky bastard! You don't just like it rough, you like it really rough. Right?"

"Something like that."

"Oh, fuck me. I've only been scratching the tip of the iceberg here, haven't I?"

"And mixing your metaphors."

Brian rolled out of the bed and stalked around the room, not finding what he was looking for. Following his instincts, he opened the dresser and here it was: a long swath of fine silk. He took it out and held it up appreciatively.

"I knew you were the kind of guy who'd bring a tie with him on a holiday," he said.

"I had a theater ticket."

Brian retrieved packets of condom and lube from his jeans. He walked back to the bed feeling very pleased with himself. He pulled the cover completely off the bed. Carl looked back at him, eyes narrowing and cock twitching. Something about him totally brought out Brian's pushy, assertive side. Throwing the foil packages on the bed, he bent down and with a quick, strong movement flipped Carl on his stomach. Straddling him, Brian forcefully took the older man's wrists, crossed them behind Carl's back, and bound them with the silk tie.

Brian leaned his bulkier frame over Carl, trapping Carl's immobilized arms between them.

He bent his head close and spoke into Carl's ear with the deepest, most authoritative tone he had. "I can't give you exactly what you need, but I can give you a hard fuck that will stay with you for days."

Carl's fingers stretched between them, desperately seeking contact. Brian's hardening cock took notice. He wedged it in the crevice between Carl's buttocks, sliding it forward and back a few times.

Brian went on. "Or I could leave you here, high and dry all night. It's your choice."

Carl grunted angrily and tried to push himself up, but Brian entwined his legs with Carl's and held him still. "I promise you I will fuck you hard and long and won't let you come till you want it so bad that a brush of my hand will set you off. In exchange, you promise to go back to bovine country, and ask this guy...what's his name?"

"Robert."

"You ask Robert out, wine and dine him, and then take him home and make him own your ass. Show him your dungeon as well."

"I don't have a dungeon."

"Whatever. Promise!"

There was a stubborn silence, so Brian sank his teeth into the fleshy part of Carl's shoulder. At the same time he resumed rocking his hips against Carl's ass.

"Oh fuck! I promise!" came Carl's muffled cry.

"Good, baby. I guarantee you'll feel my cock in you long after I'm gone."

Brian got off the bed, pulling Carl to its edge. He arranged Carl in the pose he wanted. He did just as he'd promised; he fucked Carl with rough, merciless determination. Every fiber of Brian's being focused on making Carl tremble and moan, to beg and whimper with fevered frustration. He brought Carl to the edge several times and back. He marked Carl's beautiful lean body with his teeth and hands. And when Carl was reduced to a sweaty, quivering mass, and Brian himself teetered at the edge of his self-control, he brought them to a primal, howling orgasm.

They parted ways the next morning like two old friends. Brian had kept his word, and he hoped Carl would too.

THE FERRYMAN

Gregory L. Norris

Sunlight, brilliant and blistering, spilled through the damaged bulkheads, one fraction of a second ahead of a wall of exquisite pain. The searing blast engulfed Lieutenant Junior Grade Cole Rader. Gunmetal gray tattooed in rivets evaporated in blinding-bright memories of Cape Cod in the summer; the strangely scaled trees, windblown into flat natural topiaries along the shore, and lazy rides in his skiff.

Recent dreams and fantasies about John Yuzzino superimposed over the sunny, two-dimensional vision. John, with his perpetual five o'clock shadow and neat, dark hair going silver just above the ears. And how John would look bare-chested, his bare legs and feet in a jaunty pose beneath the sun, on Cape Cod, in the skiff with Cole, his flesh glistening with sweat, a happy smile hanging crooked on his mouth, his eyes seeing Cole, only Cole, in the sunlight raining down from a cloudless sky the color of comfortable denim.

And then Cole was in the frigid, dark water. When he broke

the surface, the USS *Liberty* lolled tall above him, her super-structure clearly showing the fresh wound dealt to her above-water hull amidships. Noxious gray smoke roiled out of the impact site; dirty orange tongues licked at the exposed sinew from within, the source of that false sunlight Cole had imagined, dreaming it into lines of sweat dripping down treasure trails, masculine muscles glowing gold under dreamy August sunlight half a planet away. The explosion had blasted him out of the *Liberty* and into the Arabian Sea, only the water was too dark, too cold, even in the shadow of the damaged escort vessel.

"Boat, ahoy," Cole called, his voice echoing with an empty, eerie resonance over the waves.

The *Liberty* receded farther beyond a veil of mist and smoke.

"Ahoy! Someone, help me!"

Water lapped at Cole's ears and lips, the expected brine completely absent. The surf smelled and tasted fresh. As dead as it felt around him, Cole also sensed it was alive, undulating, teeming with energy if not actual life. Panic attempted to seize hold of him. He silenced the voices in his head attempting to steer him toward greater danger and focused. He needed to get out of the water, to return to the *Liberty*, where the promise of help was certain. His eyes locked onto the accommodation ladder running down the side of her hull, he kicked out and cut across the choppy surf.

Ignoring the weight of his shoes and socks, his service uniform, too, attempting to drag him under the water, Cole reminded himself that he'd grown up at the beach. He both respected and feared the water in healthy doses, even this body that had stolen the identity of the Arabian Sea, and maintained his levelheadedness. At least at first.

The mass and superstructure of *Liberty* receded, becoming

less distinct with each stroke despite Cole's best effort. He cut water, paddled. On the next stroke, his hand struck something cold, solid. An instant later, he was sitting in the ferryboat, in full dress uniform, staring at an ominous figure seated aft with its bony hand on an old-school wooden rudder. A man, or what looked like one, shaped and colored like a cloud, his image unleashed a chill over Cole's flesh. Cole fought the urge to shiver, failed. By the time the shudder tumbled, the ghost-form had solidified into a set of eyes, preternaturally gray between the dark fabric of a hooded cloak. Beyond, USS *Liberty* abstracted, more of an apparition now than the presence across from Cole.

It's Charon, thought Cole. *The Ferryman.*

Only it could not be. Willing the image away didn't exorcise it. Cole forced his palsied lips to move. Somehow, getting words past them proved to be more Herculean a task than any other act of training or crisis he'd soldiered through in life.

"You," he eventually said, his throat desiccated to desert. "Ferryman."

The specter's gray gaze locked with his. "Me," a deep, male voice answered.

"Where are you taking me?"

"To the other side. Though you already know this."

Another shiver tumbled down Cole's spine, equal parts ice and heat, the latter sensation somehow worse. When the landscape stabilized, Cole's dress whites glowed against the palette of moody grays, the perfect attire for a naval funeral.

"I'm not ready," Cole said. And then he shouted the same statement verbatim in anger.

The ferry drifted forward, heedless of his protest. *Liberty* was still visible, but barely, a phantom set against a pale gray sky.

"Did you hear me?"

The Ferryman nodded. "You and everyone else who's ever

joined me in this ride across the Styx. Bolder souls than you have voiced similar words, heroes every one—John F. Kennedy, Amelia Earhart, Harvey Milk, Martin Luther King. Charlemagne, David, and a thousand other kings. Men and women who weren't afraid."

"I'm not afraid of you," Cole lied.

"No, but you're afraid of *yourself*."

The retort caught him so completely off guard that the façade of Cole's anger evaporated. "What the hell does that mean?"

A humorless chuckle sounded from within the dark cowl of Charon's cloak, which fluttered like wisps of smoke, diaphanous in the gray breeze. "First, it was your family that kept you living a lie, and then that ridiculous Don't Ask, Don't Tell. The soldiers I met so long ago in Athens would have laughed at so outlandish a conceit. Do you really think the Powers of the Universe frown upon the love shown between human males? Some of the noblest and bravest warriors in history shared their beds and their hearts with other men."

Eyes narrowed, Cole shrugged, shook. "You don't know me. You don't know what I've been through."

"Don't I?" the Ferryman taunted.

The phantom tending the rudder tipped a pallid hand toward the water at starboard. Cole glanced over the rail and saw himself floating in the turgid surf, burned and bleeding, dying. His eyes connected with his other self's and, in that brief, bottled reflection, he saw all that had been lost.

Cole blinked, and he was on the skiff again, on the Cape, with John Yuzzino. Sunlight glinted. Sweat flowed. A scene from a happy life that hadn't been allowed to play out and might never now unfold. An alternate reality. Heaven, perhaps.

"Cole," John said. Only he was *Johnny* here, a laid-back

surfer dude with eyes like twin sapphires, and though the sun in the sky had created the conditions for this resplendent day, it orbited Johnny Yuzzino. He was its master, a chariot driver stretched out in a jaunty pose, his hairy legs crossed at the ankles, arms behind his head, his neck resting on wrists.

A cocky smirk broke across his unshaved mouth, crooked on one corner. The smirk revealed a length of clean white teeth, that one element lending Johnny a wolfish look more than all the hair, muscle and jeweled gaze combined. Sunlight pooled in the sweat on his taut abdominal muscles, in the hair on his legs and in the nests of dark fur exposed in the pits of his arms.

Cole's flesh ignited at the image of the other man, dressed only in loose-fit summer jam shorts, navy with white piping. He drew in a desperate breath of air heavy with the incredible male scent of Johnny, sweat and the trace of excited masculine hormones leeching through skin. Cole's arousal ran deeper through his blood, past his bones, and into his soul. Even Johnny's big feet, angled over the edge of the skiff, excited him with hunger that that part of a man's body wasn't supposed to inspire, but in this case did.

"Hey," Cole sighed.

"Come over here," Johnny didn't so much ask as order.

Cole navigated to the skiff's stern, where Johnny radiated with the sun's captured light. The skiff rocked, and the gentle dark blue surf off Cape Cod on this perfect day whispered against the hull with soft, wet giggles.

En route, he caught his reflection in the water: his chestnut hair clipped short in military style, a day or so worth of prickle on his chin, cheek and neck. Unlike Johnny's chest, Cole's was bare of fur save for the treasure trail cutting him down the middle, making a roundabout ring at his belly button. His cargo shorts, riding low on his hips, showed plenty of waistband and an inch or more of his black boxer-briefs. The waistband, in kind, flashed some curl at its very top.

Cole's legs matched Johnny's in terms of hair and muscle, those of an athlete, strong without being too showy at the calves and thighs. Big bare feet, a growing swell under that line of pubic shag, and healthy summer sweat completed an impressive image, though it was the smile on Cole's face, drifting in the waves, that was the most telling facet of this happy alternate reality.

He forced his eyes back into the boat. Despite the day's warmth, a shiver spilled down Cole's spine. Johnny.

"Fuck," he sighed, lost his balance, and fell into the other man's waiting embrace. Sunlight and male scent enveloped him, along with Johnny's arms. In that instant of energy, sweat, and radiant joy, the last of Cole's doubt evaporated. Johnny moved to kiss him, and Cole met him halfway. The contact was electric, euphoric. He gasped a breathless expletive around Johnny's mouth and swore again when his cock, swollen to its hardest state, attempted to join arms and lips in connectivity.

Legs scraped together. Big bare feet rubbed at the toes, ankles and insteps. While kissing, Johnny laced his fingers around Cole's and then tongues mimicked. Cole boldly reached his free hand down and shook the meaty fullness between the other man's legs. Johnny moaned into his mouth. His tongue licked across Cole's teeth.

"Do it, dude," Johnny said. "I've been waiting so long for this. Too fucking long."

Cole pulled back, a space of a few inches. "I didn't know."

"You didn't?" Johnny sighed, the smile on his face melancholy at the edges. "Maybe I need to be clearer." He leaned up and crushed their mouths together. "I love you, Cole Rader. Have, secretly, since our first tour together."

"No way," Cole said.

Johnny caressed his cheek and then proved his love in actions as well as words.

They maneuvered into position, that perfect mathematical male equation, with one's mouth aimed at the other's cock. Not waiting for permission, because none was required, Cole worked down Johnny's board shorts, worried his own dick might accidentally bust its load before Johnny finished freeing him from his.

In a daze, Cole absorbed the vision of the other man's nakedness, his cock first, a column of erect muscle thickest at the middle of its shaft, capped by a classic helmeted head wreathed in foreskin. Like his sweat, the lone drop of Johnny's precome had captured the sun's light. Moisture glistened in his cock's fleshy noose. It was, Cole thought, the most magnificent sight to young yet wise eyes that had traveled the globe as part of the U.S. military.

But that snapshot of Johnny's dick only occupied the top spot until he wiggled free of his shorts, and the two balls hanging loosely in a hairy sac appeared.

"Yes," Cole gasped.

Now among the other male scents were the sweat of Johnny's nuts and his patch of pubic fur. Cole inhaled, convinced he was growing high, leaned closer, licked.

"That's right, dude—suck on my rocks," Johnny urged.

Cole did, taking them into his mouth one at a time. The taste was better than he dreamed, and Cole had imagined this moment often while squirting his seed into a sock or when forced to swallow it down after lapping it off his fingers to avoid embarrassment following inspections. Worse, he'd ground his cock into his rack's miserable mattress too often while denying his needs, and the truth. The truth was he needed Johnny. Because he loved him.

"I love you, too," Cole confessed.

Opening wider, he sucked Johnny's dick between his lips, the taste hitting his tongue like liquid sunshine. All demons fled save the one that appeared without warning at the stern of the skiff where Johnny had been, a dark blemish that jumped down out of the cloudless sky and now fixed him with an ominous stare.

The taste on Cole's tongue soured. Johnny's cock was gone. So was Johnny, and he had taken the sun with him. The world again went gray around the ferry. A symphony of sad moans rose up from the swirling mists, chilling to flesh still reveling in phantom sweat.

"You?"

The Ferryman nodded. "We're almost there. It's time to pay your fare."

"No," Cole said, the weight of his full dress whites too heavy, a shroud of mummy bandages forced upon him against his will. "We didn't get to finish!"

"Woe to him who ends his mortal existence in might-have-beens and unrequited lamentations."

Cole shook his head. "*Charon,*" he growled. The Ferryman's gaze narrowed. "You called me out. You were right. I was afraid. But I'm not anymore. I want to go back. Turn around."

"That's not the way this works."

Cole broke eye contact and looked higher. The *Liberty*'s conning tower rose up from the mists, seemingly a million miles distant. "I refuse to pay."

"Then I would be forced to send you out of my ferry."

"I'll swim."

"Swim quickly," the Ferryman said. "Even I don't remember all that inhabits the Styx in this late aeon."

Cole moved toward the edge of the boat.

"And, Cole," the apparition warned. "Don't forget what you are swimming toward."

Cole tipped a final glance toward the rudder. The barest smile lit the Ferryman's face, crooked at one edge, just like...

"Johnny," Cole said, and dove into the turgid water.

Cole swam, not only for his life but also his soul. Sounds thundered in his ears, bites of noise and voices, all dissonant, none clear. Ignoring his panic, Cole pressed forward, cutting water faster and faster.

"I love you, Johnny," he whispered into the Styx. Something brushed against his leg. He ignored it, kicked, swam faster, faster yet. As fast as sunlight, he imagined. At that speed, breathing proved impossible; he forgot to anyway until the last stolen sip of air boiled in his lungs. The River Styx jellified around him, a further attempt to slow his escape. But nothing, not physics nor philosophy would keep him from reaching the safety of Johnny Yuzzino's arms.

Sea beasts splashed around him. A dense, dead fog poured down from the heavens, filled with skeletal flying things that raked at his back. Eyes shut against a hundred nightmares, Cole pressed forward, his focus on the sunlight and the source: John.

The *Liberty* rose ahead of him and pulled free of the fog. A loud, baleful horn bellowed, driving apart the mist and scattering his attackers. A klaxon answered. At first, Cole mistook it for the roar of one final sea monster, shrieking at him while in pursuit, one last barrier attempting to keep him from reaching the man he loved. Then recognition dawned—it was the ship-to-ship distress signal. The darkness broke in a blinding flash of gold.

* * *

Pain flared through Cole's body, exquisite in its agony.

"*Clear,*" a man's voice called through the cacophony of bellows and moans.

The shock hit him again. The world went dark once more before erupting in an effulgence of light. From the corona, a face appeared. Navy Physician John Yuzzino, the *Liberty's* General Medical Officer, gazed down from Heaven. Riveted gunmetal bulkheads replaced Doric columns, pearly gates and pillowy clouds as décor; instead of Ankh, Staff or Book of Life, Cole's savior held de-fib paddles in those familiar hands, which had worked such wonders in Limbo.

"Lieutenant Rader," Johnny said, his timbre rising to a desperate plea. "*Cole*, you'd better come back, buddy. Don't you leave me. Don't you fucking dare."

Cole smiled. "Never again."

Their eyes connected. No more words were spoken en route to *Liberty's* sick bay. None were necessary.

ABOUT THE AUTHORS

BEARMUFFIN has been writing gay erotica since 1985. His stories once appeared in such legendary magazines *as Honcho*, *Mandate* and *Torso*. Sadly, they are the stuff of memories. However, his fiction can now be found in anthologies published by Cleis Press, Starbooks and Bold Strokes. He loves to travel and is ever in search of grist for his literary mill.

MICHAEL BRACKEN's short fiction has been published in *Best Gay Romance 2010, Beautiful Boys, Biker Boys, Black Fire, Boy Fun, Boys Getting Ahead, Country Boys, Freshmen, The Handsome Prince, Homo Thugs, Hot Blood: Strange Bedfellows, The Mammoth Book of Best New Erotica 4, Men, Muscle Men, Teammates* and many other anthologies and periodicals.

MARTIN DELACROIX's (martindelacroix.wordpress.com) stories appear in over twenty erotic anthologies. He has published four novels: *Adrian's Scar*, *Maui*, *Love Quest* and *De Narvaez*, and three single-author anthologies: *Boys Who Love Men*, *Flawed Boys* and *Becoming Men*. Martin lives with his partner Greg on Florida's Gulf Coast.

LOU HARPER (lou-harper.livejournal.com) has misspent most of her life in parts of Europe and the U.S., but is now firmly settled in Los Angeles and worships the sun. However, she thinks the ocean smells funny. In her free time Lou stalks deviant words and feral narratives, and she is currently embroiled in a ruinous romance with adjectives. Lou is a loner, a misfit and a happy drunk.

AARON MICHAELS (aaron-michaels.com) doesn't know how to sail, but he did spend one memorable afternoon at a local marina watching sailing lessons similar to the one that inspired his story in this anthology. With any luck, the poor guy who spent more time in the water than on the sailboat that afternoon had as much fun as the characters in "Sailing Lessons." Aaron's short fiction can be found in numerous anthologies, including *Hard Hats*, *Surfer Boys*, *Skater Boys* and *Model Men*.

EMILY MORETON's publishing credits include stories in *Chroma Journal*, *Foreigness*, *Ripple Effect*, *Necking*, *Making Contact*, *In Uniform*, *Cast The Cards*, *Naughty November*, *Pour Some Sugar on It* and *Twelve Tales of Recovery*.

JOSEPHINE MYLES (josephinemyles.com) has had her erotic short stories published in anthologies from Cleis Press, Dreamspinner Press, Torquere Press and Xcite Books, and has edited two anthologies of GLBTQ fiction. *Barging In*, her gay erotic romance novel with a canal setting, was published by Samhain in 2011.

GREGORY L. NORRIS lives and writes at the outer limits of New Hampshire. A former feature writer and columnist for *Sci Fi, the Magazine of the Sci Fi Channel* who also worked on Paramount's *Star Trek: Voyager* series, he is the author of numerous books, including *The Q Guide to Buffy the Vampire Slayer* (Alyson Books) and *The Fierce and Unforgiving Muse: Thirteen Tales from the Terrifying Mind of Gregory L. Norris* (Evil Jester Press). Visit him on Facebook and online at gregorylnorris.blogspot.com.

ROB ROSEN (www.therobrosen.com), author of the critically acclaimed novels *Sparkle: The Queerest Book You'll Ever Love*, *Divas Las Vegas*, *Hot Lava* and *Southern Fried*, has had short stories featured in more than 150 anthologies.

DOMINIC SANTI (dominicsanti@yahoo.com) is a former technical editor turned rogue whose stories have appeared in many dozens of publications, including *Hot Daddies*, *Country Boys*, *Uniforms Unzipped*, *Caught Looking*, *Kink* and several volumes of *Best Gay Erotica*. This story is fiction, though he really does get sick in a fucking rowboat.

Residing on English Bay in Vancouver, Canada, **JAY STARRE** pumps out erotic fiction for gay men's magazines and has also written steamy gay fiction for over four dozen anthologies. These include *Surfer Boys*, *Skater Boys*, *Special Forces*, *The Handsome Prince* and *Model Men*, all from Cleis Press. He is the author of two historical erotic novels, *The Erotic Tales of the Knights Templars* and *The Lusty Adventures of the Knossos Prince*.

TANNER spent his childhood on a homestead in central Alaska with no electricity, indoor plumbing or running water. Stories by

Tanner have been published in *First Hand, Drummer, Inches, Beau, Hot Shots* and many other magazines. His writing has been featured in *The Seattle Standard, The Seattle Gay News* and two Alyson Publication anthologies, and he has sold comedy material to Joan Rivers and Phyllis Diller. His novel *Men Overboard!*, a comic murder mystery set on an all-gay cruise written under the name James Brock, can be found on Amazon.com. Tanner lives in Seattle where he enjoys running water and warm porcelain.

Currently residing on the northwestern coast of the Pacific Ocean, **CONNOR WRIGHT** divides his time between writing, looking after other people's dogs and wishing that the water was warm enough to swim in. When not thinking about squid and other deep-sea denizens, he can be found at connorwrites.com.

LOGAN ZACHARY (LoganZachary2002@yahoo.com) is a mystery author living in Minneapolis, Minnesota, where he works as an occupational therapist and is an avid reader and book collector. He has a collection of his short stories coming out May 2012 called *Calendar Boys*. His stories can be found in *Hard Hats, Taken By Force, Boys Caught in the Act, Ride Me Cowboy, Surfer Boys, College Boys, Teammates, Skater Boys, Boys Getting Ahead, College Boys, Men at Noon, Monster at Midnight* and *Rough Trade*.

ABOUT
THE EDITOR

NEIL S. PLAKCY is the author of nineteen novels and collections of short stories, as well as the editor of many anthologies for Cleis Press, including *Hard Hats*, *Surfer Boys*, *Skater Boys*, *The Handsome Prince* and *Model Men*. He began his erotic writing career with a story for *Honcho* magazine called "The Cop Who Caught Me," and he's been writing about cops and sex ever since, most recently with six books in the Mahu mystery series. He lives in South Florida.